A Stillness
in the Pines

Stephanie,
who knows
what lurks
in the Pines?
Neil

Neil MacNeill

Neil MacNeill

Also by Neil MacNeill
Exit Row

A Stillness in the Pines

Library of Congress Control Number: 2023905772

ISBN: 9798392235841
Imprint: Independently published

Main cover image: www.depositphotos.com
Pinecone and branch image: CarKnack LLC

Neil MacNeill

In memory of Uncle Ted, who taught me so much about living.

Neil MacNeill

"The Pine Barrens is a wilderness of sand and pine trees 1,000 square miles in area in the central part of southern New Jersey. It's the forgotten land of the northeastern urban belt."
– *Pine Barrens*, Nancy Holt

"...the pineys began to fear people from the outside, and travellers often reported that when they approached a cabin in the pines the people scattered and hid behind trees. This was interpreted, by some, as a mark of lunacy. It was simply fear of the unknown."
– *The Pine Barrens*, John McPhee

Neil MacNeill

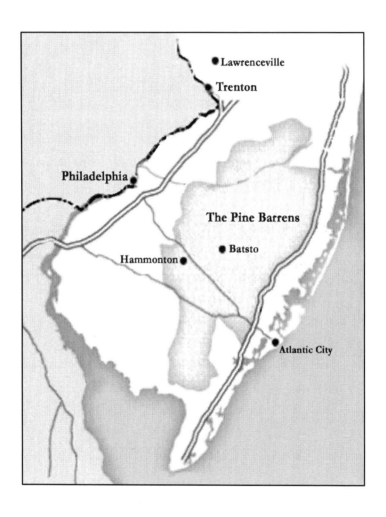

Neil MacNeill

Chapter One

So this is ground zero, where it all began. At least that's what they want us to believe. *Merda!* Now I'm starting to sound like Jimmy Lim, heaven help me.

I sure as hell don't understand all the science in this museum. I get it that a massive lightning strike made the first domino fall. Thunderstorms are pretty common in New Jersey. But all that stuff about a particle physics lab under the ground here, and a high-voltage black hole experiment? I bet the folks living in Lawrenceville didn't know *that* was going on right under their feet!

They claim it was a once in a million event. That no one could have imagined it happening. Yeah, they always say that after a major disaster. But what do I know? I'm just a stonemason from North Jersey. Gamma rays and electromagnetic pulses? All that runs off me like water off river stone.

But I do understand what happened to people.

My daughter convinced me to do this oral history for a grad student she knows, a young kid going to Rutgers. I'm supposed to tell her everything – everything I've never told anyone else. I guess I'm long overdue to confess what I did that day in the Pines. And that's a pretty strange thing for a lapsed Catholic like me to say.

This is awkward – sitting in a room in this museum, jabbering into a microphone for a kid I've never met before. Maybe it's easier with someone I don't know. She's collecting oral histories from people who lived through the event, and I can pretty much guarantee none will be like mine. What were her questions? Oh yeah, where was I, how did I react, and what did I do when the world stopped.

I can close my eyes and relive it all if I want to. But every day I try to pretend it never happened. It's been a scab in the back of my soul for...what? Seven years?

You know what happened in the cities – Philly, Trenton and New York. The acts of kindness. The chaos and riots. All the deaths, and the many, many missing. Yeah...the missing.

I was isolated when it happened. Maybe isolated isn't the right word. More like cut off from civilization, even before the "event." Have they agreed on a name yet? The Big Zap? The Sudden Nothing? The Death Pulse?

Anyhow, there were five of us in the van, six if you count J.J., the driver. He didn't speak much English. I think he understood it well enough. He was the first to go...but I'm getting ahead of myself.

I guess it would help if I told you more about me. My name is Joseph Anthony Scarapone, and I live in Middle Valley, New Jersey. I'm a stonemason, and I do all sorts of work on old buildings, stone walls and other structures in Long Valley, Califon, Hackettstown … around that area. And I'm a member of our local historic preservation commission. Which is why I was in that van in South Jersey when it all happened.

We were on our way back from a day-long seminar down in Batsto. I have to laugh – Batsto, New Jersey! The last time I was there, I was a Cub Scout on a field trip. We were bussed there to see some sort of living history presentation. You know, where guys dress up in Colonial outfits, and women all have long skirts and their hair pinned up. It was blazing hot and humid that South Jersey day when I was a kid. It seems ages ago now.

Funny, but I didn't give a rat's ass about history when I was a kid. All I really remember from that trip was trying to imagine what the women were wearing under those long, heavy skirts. That, and competing with my cousin, skipping flat stones on Batsto Lake. There was no point taking on Tony, though. He always seemed to win, no matter what we did.

But back to that October afternoon that's burned into our memories. The six of us were in this van. We were a mixed lot, if you know what I mean – a real melting pot of America – Black, White, Hispanic, Asian. I guess that's New Jersey. All of us were tired after a day of talks by the state preservation office, so there wasn't much chit-chat as we headed north, back to the park-and-ride and our homes. We had met for the first time on the ride down that morning, and talked a bit during breaks, but we hadn't really socialized. We all came from different towns in the county, and it was the county that paid for our transportation down to Batsto in that 12-passenger van – plenty of room for us to spread out and not get in each other's faces.

We had a good two-hour trip ahead of us heading north. And I guess at some point, J.J. got a traffic alert on his phone about a bad accident on Route 206. He started looking for an alternate route, taking all these back roads, and I do mean back roads. Most of them had no centerline. Tall, scraggly pine trees lined each side. No houses in sight. They don't call it the Pine Barrens for nothing!

I'm betting he lost his cell signal the further he drove. No cell signal means no navigation. And there are plenty of dead zones in South Jersey.

"Dead zone" – nice term, isn't it? You've heard about the Mafia hits down there? That's because there are no towns…thousands of acres of woods…no electronic reception. So no way the Feds could track a cell phone. It's so remote, and with all the swamps and undergrowth, the cops will never find some of the bodies. Look, I'm Italian-American, so I'm allowed to talk about the mafia – *capisci*? Anyhow, once we were deep in the Pines, good old J.J. was never going to be able to navigate out.

And then, of course, everything stopped. You know that part, but it was different for the six of us in that van. We were in middle-of-nowhere South Jersey, and we didn't have a clue what had happened. For all we knew, the Martians had landed in Grover's Mill and they'd zapped all the powerplants and cell towers. I mean, we just didn't have any idea, and we had no way of finding out. Everything just stopped. The van, our phones, our watches. They all died.

I'm sure you've read the articles in the *Times*, the *Post* or the *Inquirer*, and watched those CNN specials. But this was different for us. It was like that old *Twilight Zone* episode – what was it called? "The Monsters on Maple Street"? You know, where the aliens kill off the power in a small town and everybody starts fighting with each other. Get it? *We* were the monsters.

Stranded in the Pines, our little group of six souls was like some kind of sociology experiment...about what people will do when the shit hits the fan. We all started the day with our prejudices – some kept in check, some not – our own points of view about what's right and wrong with the world. By the time we got out of the Pines, those of us that did, we were changed. I won't say traumatized, but that fits, too.

After all these years, this oral history is a good way for me to confess. Some people might say I have blood on my hands. That's not true, at least not really. And others might call me racist or a coward. *Minchiate!* Well, you be the judge.

Okay, here goes, from the beginning.

Neil MacNeill

Chapter Two

Lila Johnson was the first to speak up when J.J. started driving down those deserted Pine Barren roads.

"Excuse me. Mr. Driver?" That got no response. She tried again.

"I said, Mr. Driver!" She raised her voice above the road noise. J.J. must have heard her, but again, he didn't reply. Lila was a big woman, and when she got her dander up, you paid attention. She was sitting a couple of seats behind J.J.

"Yo, driver!" This time, she yelled.

J.J. ignored her. He had one hand on the steering wheel and the other holding his smartphone, waving it around to get a signal.

She hauled herself up out of the seat, and walked up the narrow aisle to stand right next to J.J. "I said, driver, whatever your name is, just where do you think you're taking us?"

He kept trying to get a signal on his phone, keeping his eyes on the road and not on Lila. "*Sin teléfono tampoco. No hay señal.* Phone is no good." He finally glanced at Lila and shrugged. I doubt J.J. weighed more than 120 pounds soaking wet – he was rail-thin – but he didn't seem to be intimidated by her.

"Maybe you need to turn this van around and get us out of these woods and back to civilization, huh?" Lila placed her feet apart and put her hands on her hips. Despite the rocking motion of the van, she was solid. Picture Aretha Franklin, with a few more pounds on her, singing, "Think about what you're trying to do to me." Know what I mean?

J.J. kept driving, shaking his head and waving that phone around. For a minute, I thought Lila was going to swat it from his hand.

Adelaide joined the discussion. "She's right, you know." I looked back and forth between J.J. and Lila up front, and Adelaide Quinn, sitting in back. At first glance, Addy reminded me of my first-grade teacher – long gray hair pulled back in a tight ponytail, thin but pretty face, and posture so straight you'd think she had a 2 x 4 up her butt. As it turns out, that first impression was way off. No matter, I didn't want to get in the way of either of these two women.

J.J. got the message. With a sigh, he pulled the van over to the side of the narrow two-lane, scraping an outside mirror on pine branches as we came to a stop on the sandy shoulder.

And then it happened. There was no sound. I didn't feel anything, like some people said afterwards. But the engine died, and it got real quiet. J.J. put the transmission in Park and tried to restart the engine. There wasn't even a click from the starter. No blinking dashboard lights, either. He stared at his phone, but its screen was black and it was as silent as the engine.

"What the..." Jimmy blurted out.

We all pulled out our phones and kept touching the screens to try to make something happen, as if the harder we pressed, the more likely the stupid things would come back to life. While the rest of us were trying to resuscitate our phones and smart watches, J.J. popped the hood and got out of the van.

"This is a whole lot worse than a dead battery," I said, stating the obvious.

Jimmy pressed his face against the van's window. "Is there a military base nearby? They could be testing a directed-energy weapon – an HPEM." Leave it to Jimmy to come up with some wild-ass theory.

Evelyn looked up from her phone. "What's HPEM?" She was sitting next to Jimmy.

"High-Powered Electro-Magnetics," Jimmy said, as if everyone should have known this.

I rolled my eyes and decided to join J.J. I was pretty good at fixing my old pickup truck and cement mixer, so I thought I might be able to get the van restarted.

Stepping outside, I was struck by how quiet it was. Other than the tick-tick-tick of the cooling engine, there was nothing – no birdsong or the usual rising and falling drone of insects you hear in the Pines.

J.J. stood in front of the open hood, gazing down at the engine with a frown on his face. I took a closer look, but it was all foreign to me. Everything was covered with plastic shields and sound insulation. It was hard to see anything that even looked like an engine.

"Turbo-diesel hybrid, isn't it?"

J.J. and I both jumped at the sound of Adelaide's voice. Not only didn't I hear her come up behind us, but I was even more shocked to hear her talk about the engine. No, I'm not being sexist. She just, well, I just didn't expect it from someone like her, that's all.

"If it was just a diesel, I could probably get it going again." She glanced over at us and then back at the mysterious plumbing under the hood. "I grew up on a farm in Virginia, and I used to help my daddy keep the farm equipment running." She shook her head. "It's the hybrid-electric aspect that has me puzzled. I'm afraid I have no familiarity with that."

I couldn't stop the smirk from growing on my face. As if any of us were familiar with any "aspect" of a turbo-diesel electric hybrid!

I edged over to the side of the engine bay until I found something I recognized – a fuse block. "Maybe there's something obvious here." I pulled the plastic cover, looked for one of the larger blade fuses, and yanked it out. Holding it up to the light, I could clearly see it was blown. "Well, here's one fuse that's shot." Adelaide came over to see for herself, so I handed her the fuse.

I was about to pull another fuse when I heard a strange whistling noise above the trees. It was like some sort of video-game sound effect, and it was getting louder. "Is that a plane or..." The thought escaped my lips before I could make any sense of what we were hearing.

The tree cover was so dense, we could only see a thin

slice of sky directly overhead. But a quick shadow flashed across the pavement, and I could just make out the cross-shaped silhouette of a big jetliner.

"Why don't we hear the jet engines?" Adelaide's voice was little more than a whisper, but we both knew something was wrong.

Then we heard a thunderous crash, miles away but loud enough to shake the windows in our van.

Neil MacNeill

Chapter Three

I should've known the Pines better than most people. I grew up about an hour from where we broke down that day. When I was a kid, we'd go exploring in the woods every summer day, and even on spring and fall weekends. My cousin, Tony, and I would find old trails or make new ones. We'd search for Indian arrowheads buried in the soil or maybe hack down a dead tree, just to see it fall.

It's been too many years ago now. I've changed. The world has changed – beyond measure. But the Pines? Change doesn't come to the Pine Barrens. That place could be stuck in any time – now or hundreds of years ago, or maybe even hundreds of years in the future. I always had the sense that you could walk deep into the Pines and there'd be a good chance you'd be the first human ever to trod on that particular plot of earth. It'd be the first time in all of history that anyone had set foot there. Nobody lives in the Pines. Nobody really ever goes there.

But, of course, that's a lie.

What brought back all the old memories were the smells – the scent of pine and cedar in the air, the mossy smell of a freshwater stream somewhere nearby, and maybe a hint of rotting vegetation or even a decomposing animal not far off the road from where we were stranded. But now the wind brought the acrid odors of scorched metal and burning plastic and something far worse that I didn't want to think about. The whole group was out of the van, all of us trying to look past the treetops at the distant billowing cloud of smoke.

"Holy shit. Holy shit. That plane crash!" Jimmy Lim didn't say it, but what I was thinking was, *Another 9/11*.

"This is a whole lot more than a broken down van." Lila shook her head. I think she was starting to cry. "This is a terrorist attack. We're under attack. Again."

The wind shifted, blowing the unnatural smells of the plane crash away from us. We stood there, slack-jawed, staring at the huge plumes of blue and black rising into the evening sky. I'm not a good judge of distance, but I guessed it was only a few miles away.

"There's going to be a forest fire."

We turned to look at Eve – that's Evelyn Jesko. I need to get her name right … for posterity. How do I describe Eve without sounding like a dirty old man? She was very attractive in that girl-next-door way – black-framed glasses and long blonde hair pulled back behind her ears and held up with some kind of barrettes. She was the youngest in our group, early 20s, I'd guess, and … oh … how do I say this nicely? Ha! My Uncle Phil had a saying: Built like a brick shithouse with every brick in place. I guess that's brick-layer's humor for you.

"Fires in the Pinelands burn very hot," Eve continued. "There's a process called fuel continuity. First, the blaze ignites the dead leaves and fallen pine needles, then the sheep laurel and wild blueberry bushes around the pitch pines catch fire. The heat builds up until the sap actually boils. This time of year, a small brush fire can turn into a real inferno."

"How do you know all that?" Jimmy wasn't exactly challenging her, but then he never took anything at face value.

"My cousin was in the forest service here. I learned a lot from him." She crossed her arms in front of her chest and raised her chin, daring Jimmy to question her further.

"I thought you were a botanist," Lila said. Always the peacekeeper, she was probably trying to get between the bickering.

"I'm a molecular biologist. I specialize in disease- and drought-resistant crops. My ... my only field experience was in Kansas. Not in South Jersey." Eve paused to look at Jimmy. "I'm just telling you what I've heard – about wildfires in the Pines. If the wind is right, there's nothing to stop them."

The only one of our group who wasn't taking part in this conversation was J.J. I don't know if he followed it or if he was just thinking about more practical things. When we fell silent, J.J. shook his head and muttered something under his breath. He walked back to the van, reached in behind the driver's seat, and put on a windbreaker and cap. He pointed up the road as he turned to address us. "*Vamos a buscar ayuda.*" With that, he walked away, heading in the general direction of the plane crash.

I searched the faces of our small group, hoping that someone had a clue what he'd just said.

"He's going to get help," Lila explained. "Don't any of you speak Spanish? I thought that was required in school."

"I do," Eve mumbled, looking down at her feet. "I understand it."

"And aren't any of you going to go after him…or go with him? Huh?" Lila threw up her arms, as if asking the Lord for patience.

I guess we were all trying to figure out what was going on and what we could do. J.J. at least took some action. I'm not sure what he hoped to do or where he thought he might get help, but at least he did something. The rest of us – me included – seemed paralyzed, standing on the side of that narrow country road next to a dead van.

"So, we're royally screwed." Jimmy's eyes were glued to the angry clouds rising above the tree line.

"It's not that bad." I guess it was a dumb thing to say, but that's what came out of my mouth.

"Don't you get it?" Jimmy turned to us and let out a breath. "This is another terrorist attack. But not like 9/11. This is bigger." We all just stood there, silent. It dredged up long-buried memories of 2001 and where I was when the Twin Towers came down. For folks in Northern Jersey, 9/11 was a real gut-punch. We all knew someone who was supposed to be in the city, but simply by chance, didn't go that day. We also knew of friends and coworkers who weren't so lucky. "It's a Black Sky Event, and we're stuck here in Deliveranceville, New

Jersey," Jimmy said. "We have no idea when anyone is going to realize we're here. We can't exactly call AAA. Hell, we can't call anybody. We pretty much can't do anything."

"I don't know what a Black Sky Event is, but well, I think you may be jumping to conclusions." Adelaide's tone was gentle. I thought she had a good point. As we were all standing there on that day, none of us knew what made our van die or what hit our phones and watches – little more than paperweights now – and, of course, what brought that plane down. It was easy to assume terrorism. "Something devastating has happened – obviously," Addy continued. "But we don't know what, or how widespread it is or …" She shook her head as her voice trailed off.

"Look. It all adds up." Jimmy was getting riled, pacing back and forth in front of us. "The van dies. Our phones and watches die. We see a plane fall out of the sky and crash in the woods. It's an EMP!"

"What's an ambulance crew got to do with this?" It was Lila's turn to try to make some sense of Jimmy's ramblings.

He stopped pacing and looked at her, slowing his breathing. "EM*P*...'P' as in pulse." You could see the retired school teacher in him, searching for a way to get his point across. "Did you ever hear of Project Starfish Prime?"

He didn't wait for an answer because I guess the looks on our faces made it pretty obvious.

"In 1962, we blew up a nuke in the upper atmosphere. This was way out in the Pacific, far from any inhabited islands. By all accounts, the test was successful, but 800 miles away, in Hawaii, radios and TVs failed and a low-orbit communications satellite stopped working. It even blew out some streetlights." He paused to see if we were following all this. "The gamma rays from the blast fried all the electronics."

"So, you're saying there was some kind of nuclear explosion over New Jersey?" Eve's tone was beyond skeptical. Fists on hips, her head shaking back and forth, she looked like she was ready to cry "bullshit" at any moment.

"I don't know what caused this electromagnetic pulse – this EMP," Jimmy said. "If it was an atmospheric nuke, yeah, we would have seen it and heard it, that's true. Maybe it was some incredible space weather, like a huge solar flare, or even a military exercise gone bad. Isn't Fort Dix somewhere around here?" He paused, glancing at each of us in turn. "Only a massive EMP could have caused all of our electronics to die and the aircraft's computer systems to fail at the same time. One way or another, this was definitely a Black Sky Event."

We grew silent, each in our own mental space. Me? I looked around, taking in our surroundings. At another time, or maybe in other circumstances, some might have even called our setting pretty. A few oak trees were sprinkled among the pines, and the undergrowth was thick with greenery. We'd already had a few cool evenings, so the godawful South Jersey mosquitoes were absent, and the air was fresh and clean – except for the occasional whiff of oily stench from the plane crash, that is. Yeah, I'm kind of nuts for mentioning it, but that's how I looked at things at the time. The Pines aren't beautiful in the way the mountains of upstate New York are, or maybe the shore at Cape May, but the area has its own beauty if you take a moment to really look at it.

"Well, black sky, blue sky, whatever this...this situation is or isn't, we've got to get organized." Lila strode up to the front of the disabled van and reached out her arms, waving her hands like a preacher gathering her flock. "It's going to be dark in another hour or so, and we've got to figure on spending the night here."

"You've got to be kidding me," Eve blurted out.

Jimmy was more confrontational. "Who died and made you queen?"

Did I mention what Eve was wearing? She had on tight blue jeans and some sort of dress sandals with a bit of a heel. Her orange blouse had kind of puffy sleeves. I don't know fashion, but it all looked good on her.

And Jimmy? Well, he was a retired history teacher, and he looked the part. Where he got all this Black Sky stuff was beyond me. He probably spent more time reading crazy conspiracy theories on the internet than he did studying the American Revolution, though. And his first reaction to everything was always negative. So he wasn't about to let Lila take charge without a fight. But he obviously didn't realize what a force of nature she was.

She stepped closer to him – right into his personal space – and gave him a hard stare. "Jimmy, how about you get that chip off your shoulder and let's see how we can work together to get through this...this situation." He frowned but didn't say another word. Lila turned to Eve, her tone softer. "Honey, you don't look like you're equipped to spend a night in the woods, but that's what we're gonna have to do. So buck up. Okay?"

I was fine with Lila taking charge – somebody had to. "As long as the wind doesn't shift, I don't think the fire from that plane crash is going to come our way," I said. Maybe I was trying to reassure everyone … including myself.

"Hmm." Lila's response made me think she had her doubts. "Now let's see if we can figure out a course of action and divide up some duties. In this kind of situation, first priorities are food, water and shelter, right?"

You could tell she was an office manager, used to delegating workloads. She was thinking out loud. Even though we were about as far from an office environment as anyone could imagine, what she was doing made sense.

"There's some water bottles in the van," she said, "and since Covid, we all have plenty of hand sanitizer, right? The van will do for shelter, but we should see if there's some sign of life nearby. Jimmy. How about you do a little reconnaissance work for us?"

"What do you mean?"

"Take a walk up the road." Lila pointed in the direction J.J. had gone. "See if there's maybe a house, a gas station or a bigger road that intersects this one. Maybe you'll even see someone you can ask to get help."

Jimmy shook his head. "By myself?"

"Lions and tigers and bears, oh my!" Eve blushed the moment the words left her lips. I think she was more embarrassed than Jimmy by her taunt.

Lila turned her attention to Eve. "You know, honey, you've got a point. We should pair up. Why don't you go with Jimmy. The two of you can work out your differences along the way."

Eve let out a forced laugh, then lowered her eyes. She was smart enough to realize we had to cooperate with each other. With a quick shake of her head, she turned to Jimmy, her voice softer than before. "Yeah, alright. Let's go then. But let me get my jacket and purse."

Jimmy's lips were tight, but he also gave in. "I'll get my jacket, too, and my pouch. I've got a survival tool in it."

"What's a survival tool?" I was thinking of maybe a Swiss army knife or a Leatherman, but then realized that Mr. Conspiracy Theory would probably have something more interesting.

"It's a little metal multi-tool that has a saw blade, a knife edge, a few wrench holes," he said. "You can even break auto glass with it, and it's only the size of a credit card."

I shrugged, but filed this information away in my mind. Maybe a "survival tool" would be just what we needed at some point.

"Joseph?" Lila turned to me. No one but my mother or the nuns in school ever called me Joseph. "You pair up with Adelaide and walk back down the road."

I turned to look in the direction we'd come. The shadows from the branches made it hard to see anything other than a gradual bend in the road. "So, what are *we* looking for?"

"Anything that might help us!" Lila threw up her

hands as if talking to a child. "We all have to think creatively now. Look for a source of water. Look for a building or structure that we might have passed. Look for someone who lives here. Look for some firewood."

"Firewood?" Eve sounded incredulous. "Don't we have enough to worry about with, you know, the fire from that plane crash?"

"I'm talking about building a campfire that will give us some warmth this evening. It may get cold – it *is* October. And maybe if there's someone looking for us, well, it will help them find us. I'm sure there's a fire extinguisher in the van."

"And what are *you* going to do?" Jimmy wasn't done pushing back.

"I'm going to scour through that van and see what kind of tools I can find, plus probably a first-aid kit – to be safe. Maybe there's a space blanket in there – something to make our night in the woods more bearable."

"Huh!" Jimmy had to get in the last word, even if it was just a grunt. What a *chooch*.

Chapter Four

Addy and I walked down the side of the road in silence. Even though there was no sign of any cars or trucks, it just didn't seem right to walk in the middle of the road, so we kept to one side – the left, facing "traffic," just like I was taught in Scouts. It felt awkward at first, walking with Adelaide. I didn't know what to do or how to start a conversation. I glanced back a couple of times, looking at our broken-down van. Each time I looked, it seemed smaller and just, I don't know, defeated, edged up against the pine trees.

There was a lot of storm debris along the shoulder – small branches, rain-washed pebbles, dead leaves and pine needles. The sandy soil that's just about everywhere in South Jersey mixes well with cement, but I remember thinking I'd have to sift it through a screen if I wanted to make a good mortar. Hey, I'm a stonemason, so I look at sand differently than most folks. I picked up a small branch and dragged it along as we walked, making little lines in the dirt from its claw-like tips.

"So … Joe … Joseph … or Joey?" Adelaide broke the

silence.

Her personal question startled me. At the same time, talking to her was a whole lot better than thinking about how civilization was probably collapsing back home. "Joe. Please," I said. "Yeah, I noticed Lila keeps it formal, but all my friends call me Joe." I forced myself to keep up our little chatter. "And how about you?"

"Hmm? Oh, call me Addy. I never really liked Adelaide, but that's what Mom and Dad decided on." She scowled before continuing. "You can imagine what grade-school kids called me."

"What? Oh, yeah, Addy-laid. Sorry, that must have been a bear."

"Somehow we make it through childhood, though, scars and all."

Unlike some people, I don't make a point of talking about my youth, but it was easier with just the two of us out in the middle of nowhere. "For me, it was my last name – Scarapone. You know, 'Hey Joey, that face of yours could scare a pony!'"

She winced. "But I guess we gave as good as we got."

"Maybe," I said.

She glanced over at me, hesitated but then spoke. "I thought you pronounced your name Scar-a-pone?"

"Poppa was traditional Italian. He insisted we pronounce every vowel – like they do in Italy. He would always say, 'We got four vowels in our name. None of them are lazy. *Capisci*?'"

"I don't get it."

"Have you been to Italy? They don't talk like Italian-Americans, especially not North Jersey Italians. If you go to a restaurant in, say Verona, and order 'managot' they'll just stare at you. It's *manicotti*."

"Oh. I guess I never thought about that."

I couldn't tell if Addy was interested in all this, but I thought I saw a smile in her eyes, and I was on a roll. "I wanted people to say 'Scar-a-pone,' you know, like Patti Lupone. I guess I wanted to be more American…not to mention steering away from that 'scare a pony' crack."

She smirked. "Well, I never had that problem with Quinn."

That got a laugh out of me. But soon, all my dark thoughts drifted back. I was about to say something when Addy stopped. "What is it?"

"Look over there – in the woods."

"Okay…a bunch of pine trees and some scrub oak. It's the woods. What's up, Addy? What do you see?" I was already comfortable calling her Addy.

She put up a hand to shield her eyes, turning her head this way and that to get a better view. "There's a clearing in there, I think, or maybe a meadow…I don't know, maybe about a hundred feet or so in."

I still didn't see anything that stood out.

"It's a break in the foliage. Let's take a closer look." She started to walk into the woods.

I wanted to go along with Addy, but not before taking some precautions. "Wait," I said. I took the branch I'd been carrying and laid it across the middle of the road. Then I used my foot to make a rough arrow in the sandy soil by the roadside.

"What are you doing?"

"If we're going into the Pines, I want to mark this

spot. Just in case."

She scrunched up her face.

I let out a breath, but decided I should tell her what I was thinking. "When I was a kid, I got lost in the woods one evening." I paused, suppressing a shiver. "I thought I'd remembered a path that led to a little stream. As it got dark, everything looked the same … and I guess I lost my sense of direction."

Addy smiled and shrugged. "Okay, we'll mark our way in, breaking off branches or something. Is that alright?"

I knew that breaking off branches wasn't going to be much help, but I didn't want to look like a *timido* – another put-down from my youth – so I joined Addy as we made our way into the underbrush, heading toward this clearing she'd seen. It was harder going than it first looked. Fallen trees sometimes blocked our path, and Addy made the mistake of stepping *on* one instead of climbing over it. The moss and lichen on the dead tree were slippery as axle grease. She waved her arms to catch her balance, and I rushed to steady her before she took a real tumble. As I eased her down, her face flushed. She opened her mouth to say something, but then probably thought better of it. We slowed the pace after that and tried to make our way together. The stickers and thorny briars snagged our pant legs, but we made it through with only a few scrapes and bruises. The clearing turned out to be a narrow dirt road. "I'll be damned," I said. "It's a fire road."

Addy looked up and down the sandy trail. There was nothing much to see, and it was getting darker by the minute. "Why do you call it a fire road?"

"The Forest Service carves these into the Pines so they can get equipment in here, you know, in case there's a forest fire. There were a few roads like this in the woods behind my house. When I was growing up." Except for a raggedy line of weeds down the center, this two-track looked pretty well maintained. I bent down and dug my fingers into the soil. "Hmm, sugar sand."

Addy turned to me, a question on her face.

"It's deceptive … sugar sand. You could sink up to your axles if you tried to drive down this road in a car. You'd need a 4x4 with really good tires."

She eyed the sandy road more carefully, looking along the verge that rose up on each side before the underbrush took over. "Well, it looks like there *was* a Jeep or something down here recently – look at these tire tracks."

I guess I was too preoccupied thinking about the sand to even notice, but she was right. I walked over to where she was standing and leaned down to take a closer look. The soil was still damp in places, probably from last night's rainstorm. I could make out the imprint of a tire with deep treads, the kind you'd put on your truck if you were going mudding.

When I rose up, I was standing a bit too close to Addy. I hadn't been that close to a woman since my wife left me, but I tried to put that thought out of my head. "This means that there's probably another person nearby," I said.

"Well, that or they passed through recently."

I nodded in agreement. No point getting our hopes

up. I took a deep breath, trying to figure out what to do and trying not to think about this attractive woman standing right in front of me. A few seconds passed, maybe more. I don't know what I was going to say, but it no longer mattered when we heard the shot. It was loud and close by.

She put out her arms and grabbed my shoulders. "Jesus, Joe, let's get outta here!"

Chapter Five

They say everyone has a fight-or-flight instinct. At that moment, there was no doubt which impulse took hold of us. We scrambled back through the woods, trying to head in the general direction we'd come from. I know I tripped a couple of times and I guess Addy did, too. While I have a pretty good sense of direction, the only thing I was thinking about right then was getting as far away from that gunshot as possible. Breathing hard, we came out of the woods a long way from where we went in. I was disoriented for a moment until I figured out which way to go.

"Come on! Let's get back to the van." I started to jog up the road, and Addy kept pace. But I skidded to a stop when we came to the dead branch I had placed in the road. It was still there, but it was smashed. I could smell the sour odor of my own sweat. "What the hell's going on?"

Addy's breath was ragged. "We can talk about it … when we get back … back to the van." I looked over and saw the fear in her eyes. "I don't want to stop here," she said.

The van seemed much farther away than I remembered, and the light was fading. When we finally got there, everything appeared so normal. Eve and Jimmy were setting up twigs and broken branches in the middle of the road in front of the van. Lila was wedging one of the van's jump seats out the side door. Jimmy stopped what he was doing when he saw us, a smile draining from his face. "What the hell happened to you?"

I took a good look at Addy, probably for the first time since our mad dash through the woods. If I looked anything like her, I could understand Jimmy's comment. Her well-kept bun was loose and laced with little twigs. There were scratches on her forehead and one of her pant legs was ripped.

I didn't wait to catch my breath before speaking. "Didn't you…didn't you hear the goddam gunshot?"

They were all staring at the two of us now. "We heard … something," Lila said. "I don't know, it was kind of far away. I guess I thought it was a truck backfiring or something like that."

I gave her a hard stare. "*Really*? That's it?"

Jimmy's face flushed. "Yeah, we all remarked about it," he said. "But when we didn't hear anything else, we just got back to work here, you know, building a campfire and stuff."

I shook my head. "What, are all of you *stupido*? You heard something that could have been a car or could have been a gunshot, and you did *nothing*?"

"We didn't hear anything else," Jimmy said. "One

loud crack, and that was it. So we got back to work building the fire. You know, so we can maybe not freeze tonight? Is that all right with you, big guy?"

I had to count to 10 or I would've totally unloaded on him. "Somebody shot at us, or something pretty damned close to us. Got that?"

"It was a shotgun blast," Addy said. "Didn't you think to come after us...to see if we were okay?"

We waited for someone to respond, but other than looking sheepish, no one did. I was fuming.

Addy took a breath before continuing. "We should, I don't know, be prepared for somebody stalking us or something."

Lila dropped the jump seat on the road and approached the group. "Now hold on, just hold on a minute." I could see her trying to gather her thoughts. "So, let's say it *was* a gunshot..."

"Let's not just say it – it *was* a gunshot." Addy narrowed her eyes.

"It sure as hell wasn't a backfire," I added.

"Okay, okay." Lila paced around the jump seat lying cockeyed in the road. "So ... what are we supposed to do? I can't believe there's some serial killer out here, hiding in the woods, waiting for our van to break down..."

"He was probably just hunting deer." It surprised me to hear Jimmy say something rational instead of his usual crazy conspiracies.

"But it's not hunting season," Addy said.

"So he's *poaching* deer," Jimmy replied. "It's probably a Piney. Who else lives in these godforsaken woods?"

The group fell silent. Jimmy's words didn't reassure me one bit. "Look …" I didn't want to scare everyone, but I also didn't want them to brush off the danger. "I grew up about an hour from here." I stopped and decided to take a different tack. "When I was 17, I had a run-in with a Piney."

"Run-in?" Addy raised an eyebrow. "What do you mean?"

"I had borrowed my Dad's pickup truck, and I went exploring down some dirt roads." I hesitated, but all eyes were on me now. "I drove down this fire road, like the one we saw, but it dead-ended in a field, and there was a little tar-paper shack…"

"So what's your point with this heartwarming story?" Jimmy said. I could've punched him in the nose.

"My point, *boombots*, is that a Piney was sitting on the front porch of that shack, and as I was doing my best to make a three-point turn without getting stuck, the guy sat up, grabbed a shotgun and pointed it at me."

"Oh my God," Eve gasped.

"So … did he shoot at you?" Lila asked.

"I didn't stick around long enough to give him a chance." I turned to look at each one of our group of lost souls. "My point, guys, is you have no idea what you're dealing with here." I let that sink in.

"Okay, so there's a weird old hermit who lives out here, and he has a shotgun." I could see the wheels turning in Lila's head. She must have been really good at keeping the office staff in line. "There's no reason he'd want to shoot us. I mean, we've just broken down on a public road. What have we done to bother him?"

"We're in his territory now," I said. "We don't belong here. We're trespassing."

"Well, if push comes to shove, we've got some firepower of our own," Jimmy said.

"What are you talking about?" I gave him a look, trying to figure out what was in his screwed-up head.

"Eve is carrying," he said with a smile.

Neil MacNeill

Chapter Six

My grandfather had an old .22 rifle. It was a very basic piece – no scope, and the bolt handle felt as big as a rock pick. You had to pull the bolt back and down to load one bullet at a time. Nothing worked very smoothly, including the trigger. Once I was old enough, Grandpa used to take Tony and me to the local dump – you know, the landfill. On a Saturday evening in fall or winter, the place was pretty deserted. Tony and I would scrounge through the trash to find Campbell soup cans or old coffee tins, set them up against a dirt ledge, and shoot them. The smell of gun oil on the long barrel, the heft of the wooden stock against my shoulder, and the thrill of actually clipping a can and seeing it jump as if by magic, that's all burned into my memory.

But one time Grandpa said, "*Un peccato*. No rats here. You should shoot *live* target." He laughed when he said that, an awful, rheumy laugh that made me wonder for the first time what kind of man he really was. I wish I could forget that day.

There was dead silence in the group after Jimmy

revealed Eve's secret.

Her face was bright red. "I told you that in confidence, Jimmy," she whispered.

To be honest, I was pretty shocked. Now if *Jimmy* had said he was carrying a gun ... or a big Bowie knife or ninja throwing stars ... I wouldn't have been surprised. Even Lila. I mean, she did work in downtown Newark, so I guess I could understand if she had a pistol in her purse. But Eve? It just didn't seem to fit with this beautiful young woman.

After a few uneasy seconds, Eve spoke up. "I work in New Brunswick and, well, there's been a lot of muggings and stuff at night," she said. She crossed her arms over her chest, a protective posture I'd seen her take throughout the day when she was challenged or unsure.

"Do you have a permit?" Addy's tone was mild, but direct. I guess she wanted to get a better idea of what we were dealing with. "Do you have a *carry* permit?"

"More importantly, do you know how to use the gun...safely?" Lila said.

Eve lifted her chin and gave a quick toss of her head. "Mm-hmm. It's just a little 32. I keep it in my purse."

"As in .32 caliber pistol?" Lila asked.

"Mm-hmm," Eve said. "I go to a pistol club every now and then to keep sharp." She paused and looked down, her voice softer. "It's...it's empowering."

"If that's what you need to feel empowered ..." I stopped, and put a filter on my mouth. If I blurted out what I was thinking, well, our group might've gotten even more splintered.

After this tense exchange, we all clammed up. Addy

grabbed my arm and said, "Come on, let me patch you up. You look a fright."

"Huh?" I raised a hand to my forehead and realized I was bleeding.

"Lila? Did you find a first-aid kit?"

"It's on the floor by the front seats, Adelaide," Lila said. "Leave it there when you're done, so we know where to find it."

Addy led me back into the van, and I sat down in the driver's seat. I have to admit, it's the first time I'd thought about J.J. since he'd left.

"Just sit still a minute and let me sort this out," Addy said. She propped the first-aid kit on the dashboard so she could see in the waning light, and rummaged around until she found some alcohol wipes and Band-Aids. "This will probably sting."

I did wince when she wiped the cut on my head, but tried not to let it show. As she was leaning over me, my eyes went to, you know, her partially open blouse. It was the first time I'd noticed the silver cross she wore on a little chain. I'd had plenty of time to think about crosses when I was in school – the nuns made sure of that. And in my adult experience, people who wore their religion around their necks were pretty serious about it. It was another side of Adelaide I was finding out about.

"I was thinking about J.J. just now," I said, deciding not to let her know what was really going through my mind.

"Mmm?"

"Do you think he's going to get help? I mean, he's out there on his own and, well, do you think there's anyone *else* out there …"

Addy finished taking care of my wound, stepped back, and looked at me. "You know, Joe, under your tough exterior and macho Italian quips, you're really a softy inside."

I didn't know how to take that – was it a compliment? "Yeah, I guess," was all that came out. Dumb response, I know.

She knelt down so we were eye to eye. "Look, I'm just as frightened as you are. More than that, I'm not sure about Jimmy, and I don't know what to think about Eve and her pistol. Lila's all right, I guess."

She waited for me to say something, but I just shrugged.

"My point, Joe, is I think we should stick together…you and me…kind of watch out for each other." She smiled again, and I couldn't help but smile back. "Deal?" she said.

"Okay, deal." I tried to reach out to shake hands, but instead, she kissed me on the cheek. I must have turned beet red. It was dark enough in the van, so maybe she didn't notice. Maybe. Another awkward moment with Addy. I was having a few of them.

"My turn to patch *you* up," I said and got up from the driver's seat, inching by her so we could trade places. She didn't have any cuts that required a Band Aid, so I just cleaned up the few scratches on her forehead and arms and applied some antibiotic cream. Touching someone else's skin, well, it felt so personal.

"All done?"

"Yup," I said.

"Okay, let's see about getting that fire going. It's getting chilly."

We got to work with the rest of the group – gathering branches and even logs when we could find them. I'm not sure who decided to build the campfire in the middle of the road, but it made sense. If anyone came down this lonely stretch, they'd be forced to stop and help us. We placed the jump seat up against the front bumper of the van so we could use it as a lookout point. Lila went back to double-check the van for anything else we might need, and came out clutching a bunch of water bottles to her chest. She lined them up on the shoulder of the road near the jump seat and made a point of counting out loud. "So, we've got 12 water bottles and there are 5 of us – no telling if or when J.J. is coming back," she said. "Let's figure on two bottles each, and two in reserve for, I don't know, hygiene purposes." She turned to each of us to see if anyone disagreed. "Everybody okay with that?" Even Jimmy nodded.

The last rays of sunlight reflected on beads of condensation along the van's windshield. Color was beginning to seep from the sky, and I was surprised to see a bright star overhead. I guess we were far enough away from any city lights…or more likely Camden and Philly were blacked out from whatever had zapped all our electronics. There *was* a glow in the sky, and I realized it was probably the fire from that plane crash. It didn't seem that close or threatening anymore, but it was certainly something we'd have to keep an eye on. There was a peculiar smell in the air as night fell. It reminded me of my grandparent's unfinished basement, like cement before it's had a chance to cure.

Once there didn't seem to be anything more to do, Lila gathered us together in her usual way – arms out, fingers flapping against her palms. "Come on over," she said. "Anyone here a smoker?" She looked around at each of us. "More to the point, does anyone have a lighter?"

"Um, yes." Addy spoke up. I hadn't pictured her as a smoker. Maybe that's why she was so out of breath when we were running through the woods. She caught my sideways glance. "I don't smoke tobacco," she whispered.

It took me a second to catch on. I mean, what the hell, pot's legal – is now and was then, so no biggie, right? I'm just not a smoker.

We all gathered around the pile of wood we called our campfire, looking forward to its warmth and light.

Chapter Seven

How hard can it be to start a campfire when you've got a cigarette lighter? *Gioco da ragazzi,* right? Child's play. Nope. Not even a little bit.

We had plenty of wood and debris in one form or another – leaves, twigs, pine needles and branches in a loose, airy pile with some bigger logs mixed in, but it was all pretty wet. They say there's enough water in the Pines to satisfy New York City's thirst for years – some trillions of gallons. A lot of it's below ground in the aquifers, but that evening in the Pine Barrens, a lot of water was in the firewood we'd gathered.

Addy pulled out her lighter and bent down to start the fire, but Lila stopped her before she could flick it. "Uh-uh, lady. That's not going to work."

Addy gave Lila the stink eye. I'm sure we were all pretty stressed out at that point.

"We need something other than kindling," Eve said. Now we all stared at her.

"And what do you know about starting a campfire?" Jimmy said. "What? Your cousin the forest ranger gave you some lessons?"

I have to hand it to Eve. It would have been easy just to tell Jimmy to go F himself. Ha! I had plenty of sore knuckles from nuns with yardsticks when I was in school, so "fuck" was beaten out of my vocabulary at an early age. But Eve had some biting sarcasm she could wield when she wanted to.

"If you don't mind, Jimmy," she said, "I'd like to stop listening to you now."

I got a good chuckle out of that. If it wasn't so dark, we probably could have seen Jimmy steaming.

The moment passed, and then Lila spoke up. "So, what do you suggest, Evelyn?"

"We need paper or something dry and flammable," Eve said.

The group got quiet again. I was thinking about the little pamphlets we'd picked up at Batsto Village, but that probably wasn't going to be enough.

"Why don't we siphon some gasoline from the van?" Jimmy said. "That'll get it going."

"It's a diesel, Jimmy. Diesel's not as flammable as gasoline." Addy's tone was matter of fact, but of course, Jimmy wasn't going to let it go.

"So, let's use one of the road flares. That'll ignite the diesel fuel and get those wet logs burning in no time."

"No!" Lila was adamant. "We don't want to start a conflagration here. And we need to save the flares for a real emergency. Heaven knows what's in store for us."

"What about...what about in the van?" Addy said. "In the glovebox. Is there an owner's manual?"

I didn't wait for a response from the group. I groped

my way to the driver's door in the dim light and climbed up into the van, then felt around on the dashboard until I found the glovebox, and popped it open. My hands found something that could have been a manual – it was the size of my parents' Bible. "I think I've got it!" Careful not to trip, I made my way back and knelt down by our makeshift campfire.

"Guys, if you don't mind, I'd like to set this up the way they taught me in Scouts." I waited for a response, especially from Jimmy, but got nothing, so I went to work. "I'm going to build it log-cabin style, with the larger branches set apart and smaller branches at 90 degrees on top." I called Addy over. "Join me over here and flick that lighter so I can see."

She crouched on the cold pavement next to me. I felt like I was reenacting some caveman scene. I held up the manual I'd found in the glovebox to the feeble glow from her lighter, and let out an unintelligible sound of triumph. Inside the leatherette cover were hundreds of pages of diagrams and type. I didn't care what was on the pages. All I saw was clean, dry paper. "Guys, come stand around here to block the wind." One by one, I tore the pages from the manual, crumpled them up and gathered them in a small pile under the twigs and branches. "Okay, Addy, try it now."

I might have stopped breathing for a moment as the first flickers of flame caught in the paper.

"It's working!" Addy called out. But I could feel her shoulders sag as the paper flared then died. The dark seemed even more oppressive.

Lila spoke up. "I've got some lipstick in my purse."

"What the hell's the point of that?" Jimmy said.

"It's flammable, James."

I hadn't thought of that. Thankfully, Lila had her pocketbook around her neck. She scrunched down next to Addy and me, and said, "Adelaide, I'll need some light here, please."

With one hand cupped around the lighter, Addy flicked it again, and Lila started tearing pages from the manual and spreading fat lines of lipstick across each one. "Now crumple them up and try again," she said.

I did what I was told, placing balled-up paper in the spaces between the branches, right up against the leaves and twigs.

"Go on, dear," Lila said to Addy. Her hand was shaking as she directed the lighter's flame at the paper. I cupped my hands around hers and bent down to blow on our new tinder. At first there was just smoke, but soon I heard the crack of a twig, and we had to step back as a small blaze spread to the bigger branches. We'd done it. It was the most primitive of accomplishments, but we'd done it.

"How did you know?" I asked Lila. "I mean, about the lipstick?"

She had an odd look on her face, and at first I thought she wasn't going to answer. "I have a young boy," she said. "He almost caught the house on fire one time."

"Oh." Yeah, another dumb response from me.

My eyes watered from the smoke, but I didn't care. I looked around, and everyone had little smiles on their faces, probably feeling the same sense of accomplishment

I had, or maybe reminiscing about some bonfire from their youth. Everyone except Eve, that is. She was standing kind of funny, and fidgeting, almost shivering. "What's wrong, Eve?" I asked.

She looked down at her feet and gave a quick shake of her head. "I have to pee."

Jimmy let out a guffaw. He was such a *cretino*! I felt bad for Eve, and I looked to Addy, willing her to help. By some miracle, she did.

"Come with me, Eve," she said. "I've got to go, too."

"But I can't … I mean, I've never peed in the woods." Even in the flickering light of the campfire, I could see Eve's discomfort.

"It's not hard," Addy said. "I'll show you." She went over and grabbed Eve's arm, walking to the far side of the road with her. She stopped and turned to the rest of us. "Now be polite and look the other way. We can't go in very far – it's too dark."

We all turned dutifully away from the edge of the woods where they'd gone. I felt pretty awkward, and I was trying not to think about the mechanics of girls peeing in the woods. Not just girls in general, but Addy and, of course, Eve. I tried to concentrate on the crackling sounds of our fire and let my gaze unfocus as shifting shadows and light illuminated the nearby trees. That's probably why I didn't see the single dim headlight or hear the distant sound of an engine until Jimmy cried out.

Neil MacNeill

Chapter Eight

Jimmy stepped into the middle of the road in front of the campfire, jumping up and down and waving his arms, yelling like a *pazzo* – a nut case. "Hey! Stop! Help us!" Lila and I edged past the campfire and joined him. Caught up in the excitement, I started shouting, too, signaling the driver, whoever he was, to slow down.

The engine sounded like one of my old cement mixers, a throaty pup-pup-pup. But then it got loud, like the driver was accelerating hard. The roar of the engine drowned out our cries for help. The damn thing wasn't going very fast, but it just kept coming straight at us. I raised a hand to shield my eyes from the glare of that lone headlight. Lila seemed to steel herself for a confrontation. She stood next to me, hands on hips, as if the sheer force of her will could stop it. But Jimmy? He just kept waving his hands and screaming. Heck, the campfire was behind us, right in the middle of the road. The guy *had* to stop.

When he was almost on top of us, I could make out an upright exhaust pipe and tall, knobby rear tires. It was a goddamn farm tractor! A guy in a baseball cap was driving it, and he was bearing down as fast as he could go. I grabbed Lila's arm and pulled her out of the way, stumbling back to find shelter in front of the van. Jimmy did a quick fake, like he was some kind of basketball player, then dove for cover to the opposite edge of the woods.

The tractor swerved to the right, its tires crashing through the campfire. Sparks and half-burned branches shot into the air. I lost hold of Lila as I lurched backwards, my arms cartwheeling as I tried to regain my balance. The driver over-corrected to get back on the road, and I saw a front tire leave the pavement like the thing was going to tip. It came back down with a crash.

I caught sight of movement by the edge of the woods and watched as Addy and Eve emerged on the opposite shoulder. Eve drew the .32 from her purse, racked a round as she took a shooter's stance and raised the gun in both hands. I shouted for her to stop, but I'm not sure she heard me. Addy's face was lit by the remnants of our fire. She shook her head and brought her arms down in a karate chop, striking Eve's wrists just as the gun fired. God, it was loud. I didn't hear the bullet ricochet off the pavement, but saw a small spark up the road. As the tractor disappeared into a tunnel of its own light, I saw a bulky object, like a big slab of meat, fall off the back of the tractor and bounce onto the road.

I took a deep breath. I must have been holding it for a while because I felt light-headed. My ears were ringing, maybe from the gunshot or from adrenaline. The sharp smell of gunpowder mingled with the wood smoke. Jimmy and Eve knelt by the side of the road, talking to each other. I couldn't make out their words. His arm looped around her shoulders. It all seemed to be over.

Addy came rushing over, and I opened my arms to give her a hug, grateful that we were both okay and that she'd stopped Eve from shooting the guy. But Addy wasn't coming to me. That was when I heard Lila moaning. She was sprawled on the ground next to the jump seat, a big branch from our campfire across her legs. Tiny sparks flickered on her pants. I lifted the branch as Addy grabbed a bottle and poured water over Lila's legs.

"What the hell!" Jimmy shouted and came strutting over. "Did you see that guy? He wasn't going to stop. He could've killed me."

I didn't reply until Jimmy got close. "And Eve could've killed him."

Jimmy started to say something but then he saw Lila on the ground, Addy kneeling next to her. "Holy shit, what happened?"

"A log ... she tripped ... the fire." My words weren't coming out very well. I joined Addy and put a hand on Lila's cheek, looking into her eyes. "How bad?"

"It hurts like a son of a bitch, Joseph." Lila spoke between clenched teeth.

"Do you think it's broken?"

"How the hell do I know?"

"Okay. Okay." I edged down closer to her legs. Her left leg was straight, but her right was bent at the knee. Other than some charred bits of fabric on her pants, I couldn't see anything wrong. "It's your right leg that hurts ... is that correct?"

She looked down at me and nodded.

"I'm going to run my hands down each side of your right leg. Very gently and slow."

"Yeah, you do that, white boy."

At least Lila still had a sense of humor.

"What are you doing?" Addy whispered to me. I gave her a look that I hope communicated my thoughts – shut up and let me do this. "We have to see … see if she's badly bruised or if she's got a … a fracture." Addy twisted her lips in a frown, but then nodded.

As delicately as I could, I eased my hands down her right thigh, stopping at her knee. "Lila. Can you straighten out your leg?" She nodded and slowly moved her right leg. I could see beads of sweat on her forehead. "Okay. Good." As I continued to move my hands down her right calf, I felt a big bump on her shin. She let out a cry. "Sorry." I tried to think back to my first-aid merit badge, and everything the Scouts had taught me about dealing with this kind of injury. "Can you wiggle the toes on your right foot?"

"I think so," she murmured. She closed her eyes and frowned, as if the effort was going to take every bit of her strength. After a moment, she let out a breath. "Yeah. Yeah, I can wiggle my toes. I can feel them okay." The slightest smile appeared at the corner of her mouth. "But Jesus Christ Almighty, it hurts."

"You're gonna be alright, Lila." I smiled back at her.

"Oh yeah? Where did you get your medical degree? Walmart?"

I heard Eve chuckle and turned to see her standing over us. I was still really pissed at her for firing off her gun. "Hey." I looked her in the eyes. "Make yourself useful. I've got a jacket in the van – third row back on the right." She hesitated, but then nodded. "And see if you can pull a headrest off one of the seats. For Lila."

Jimmy seemed to realize he wasn't doing anything helpful, an amazing bit of self-awareness for that guy. "I'll stoke the fire and move some of the branches closer."

"You do that, Jimmy."

When I started to stand, Addy grabbed my arm and whispered. "Did you see that … that thing that fell off the tractor?"

I nodded.

"What do *you* think it was?"

"It was something … it looked like … I don't want to think about it right now."

Neil MacNeill

Chapter Nine

Lila squirmed, moving her shoulders against the rough, sandy soil. "It hurts like hell, Joseph. God help me, it hurts."

"Okay, Lila. Try to be still. We'll get you fixed up. I promise."

Eve appeared with her arms full, and I stood, waiting for her to give me the things I'd requested. The flickering shadows of our campfire hid her expression, but I could tell by her stance that she wasn't about to just hand them over.

"I have your jacket," she said. "And I managed to pry a headrest off one of the seats." Eve paused, like she was waiting for an "atta girl" from me.

Addy picked up on her need for approval. "Nice work, Eve." She stood and took the headrest from Eve, then knelt next to Lila again. "I'm going to put this under you, to support your head. Is that okay, Lila?"

"Yes, that sounds fine, Adelaide."

With everything Lila was going through, I was amazed how civil she was. I tried to think back to my first-aid training, but nothing came to mind. Could she go into shock? Maybe hypothermia from the cold ground? Eve was still hovering nearby. "Let me have that jacket. Please." She shoved it into my hands. No love lost between the two of us, I guess. I bent down and draped it over Lila's torso, tucking in the edges to keep out the increasingly cool night air.

"You're not getting fresh with me, are you, Joseph?" A weak smile appeared on Lila's face. I took it as a good sign.

Jimmy was hanging back from the group, hands shoved into his front pockets, a blank expression on his face – inscrutable Asian, right? Eve stood next to him in her usual defensive pose. I opened my mouth to ask them something, but stopped and considered how to phrase it so I wouldn't piss them off. "Lila's being very brave, but she's obviously in lots of pain."

"Oh, I'll get by, Joseph. I'll get by." Her voice was unsteady.

"You just lie still and let your body heal," Addy whispered.

"Here's the thing." I took a breath before asking. "Do any of you have some kind of painkiller? Ibuprofen or even aspirin? Anything will help." I looked at each face in the glow of the firelight. Addy shook her head, but I wasn't sure she was being straight with me after her comment about smoking pot. Eve kind of shrugged. That could have meant yes or no. But Jimmy had an odd smirk on his face, as if he was the only one privy to an inside joke. After the longest pause, he spoke up. "I've got some oxy."

I'm sure my mouth hung open. Addy said what I was thinking. "Oxy? As in oxycodone?"

"Yup." Jimmy was totally unfazed. "It's in my survival pouch – the one I always carry with me. Everywhere I go."

"So you regularly carry around an opioid?" I asked.

"Yes, indeed." Jimmy's smile broadened. "You've got to be prepared for anything." He let that sink in, then added, "Like this, for instance." He spread his arms as if to indicate the woods, the dead van and everything.

"Get it, Jimmy." It wasn't a request. I couldn't care less what he was doing carrying oxycodone with him. I just needed to help Lila. But Jimmy wasn't about to cooperate. I gave him a glacial stare. "Please, Jimmy." Maybe I could catch more flies with honey than with vinegar. That's what my Mama used to say. But why did Jimmy and me have to have this ongoing battle of wills? Of course, he still didn't respond. *Che palle!* What balls that guy had. "What the hell, Jimmy! For Lila."

I swear he counted to 10, stock still with that stupid grin on his face before he moved, clambering into the van in the darkness.

I closed my eyes. There was so much the five of us had to work out. I heard my Mamma's voice in my head: "The mother of idiots is always pregnant!" That made me smile. I needed to get over my contempt for Jimmy or we'd end up in a real fight. Christ, I hadn't punched anyone since I was a teenager, but man, I sure as hell wanted to sink my fist into his smirking face.

Jimmy scrambled back down from the van and walked over to the campfire, keeping his back to me. I could hear him rummaging around in his precious little pouch, probably figuring out what he'd share and what he wouldn't. The clink of pills in some kind of bottle was followed by the snap of a child-proof cap. He zipped up the pouch and walked over to Lila. "This should do the trick," he said.

Addy took the pills from Jimmy and reached for another water bottle. "Are you allergic to any painkillers, Lila?"

"No, no, I don't think so. I've had some strong stuff before. I should be okay with the oxycodone, Adelaide."

Addy looked up at Jimmy. "How strong?"

"Three twenty-five milligrams each," he said, "but they're kind of old so they've probably lost some potency."

Addy unscrewed the water bottle and tilted Lila's head so she could swallow the pills. All things considered, Lila seemed to be dealing with her injuries pretty well. I'm not sure I'd be as calm.

"What else do you have in that pouch, Jimmy?"

Addy had a way of asking exactly what I was thinking, but I couldn't resist piling on. "Besides prescription drugs," I said.

Jimmy clutched the pouch to his chest. "You just wish you were as prepared as I am for a disaster...all of you."

I closed my eyes and tried to dispel the venom building inside me. I knew it was counter-productive to keep taunting that little *stronzino*. I had to call on my better angels to calm me down. With Lila hurt and a long night ahead of us, we *had* to cooperate. I kept my voice as neutral as possible. "Hey, Jimmy. What say we call a truce?"

Nothing from him. He wouldn't even look at me.

I tried again. "Jimmy. Let's stop this bullshit."

He turned to face me. "I will if you will."

He must have been bullied pretty badly when he was in school. That's all I could figure. "Right. Okay, then." I reached out to shake his hand – a sign of peace. Of course, he hesitated. He took a long look at my hand, maybe to see if it was some kind of trick. When we shook hands, I had to stop myself from showing him just how strong a stonemason's grip could be.

Addy stood to join us. "Lila seems to be resting okay now," she said.

"Good drugs will do that!" Jimmy said.

Eve let out a very unfeminine bark, and soon Addy caught the giggles. Maybe this was their way of dealing with stress, their defense mechanism, so I tried not to be the wet blanket.

"All right, boys and girls," I said, "let's gather 'round the campfire and sort a few things out." I dragged another dead branch from the roadside and placed it on top of our welcoming blaze. One by one, we sat down by the fire. I noticed we all kept to the side closest to the van and the shoulder...just in case another crazy Piney decided to crash our party.

Neil MacNeill

Chapter Ten

The summer between my Junior and Senior years in high school, I worked at my Uncle Frank's meatpacking plant in Philly. I didn't mind the long drive. Work started at 6 a.m., so traffic wasn't an issue. But I never had another job that took so much out of me. I was on my feet 10 hours. I had to wear layers to keep warm, but I ended up soaked with sweat by the end of the day.

Then there was the noise. They always played loud rock music in the plant, maybe to drown out the sounds of the overhead chains and conveyors, or so you wouldn't hear the cusswords of your coworkers, or maybe it was just to keep us all awake. It was impossible to make friends or even get to know the name of the guy standing next to you. I just put in my time and tried to keep up with the unending flow of animal carcasses. I built up some muscle that summer, but it made me realize I had to do something else with my life.

After a while, I got used to the smell of dried blood and animal fat that would linger on my skin and in my hair. Hard to find a girlfriend when you smell like a meat plant. I'd take long, hot showers when I got home, and then go out for a drive to clear my head. I usually ended up at Cedar Lake for an evening swim. There was always a bonfire and a bunch of high school friends hanging out by the lake.

The sharp smell of pine pitch from our campfire brought back those memories. Sitting next to Addy, with just the occasional snap from the fire, I felt drained. I could've nodded off, but I kept thinking about Jimmy dancing around in the roadway, and Eve shooting at that Piney, and that big slab of meat or whatever it was that fell off the tractor. How can you be dead tired and pissed off at the same time? That's what I felt, and I was glad for the silence.

We had started out as a group of six. Now J.J. was gone. And Lila was out cold. I could hear her soft snores over my left shoulder. Sleep is a great healer, and she needed it. There wasn't much more we could do for her. "*Dormi bene*," I whispered.

"What did you say?" Addy asked.

I shook my head. "Nothing, really. Just a quiet prayer for Lila."

Addy smiled. "That's nice, Joe."

It was strange how the four of us had split into couples – Jimmy and Eve a bit closer together, Addy and me separated from them by a patch of sandy soil. I guess it's natural to crave human companionship in a situation like ours.

"Didn't you think Jimmy was brave?" Eve broke the silence. "He did everything he could to stop that asshole on the tractor … even putting his own life in danger."

Jimmy let out a snort. "I was just trying to stop the guy ... but I did move fast, didn't I? Jumped out of the way just in time!"

He looked at Addy and me for a reaction. I decided to hold my peace ... that is until the next thing out of his mouth.

"That's more than you can say for Lila, huh?"

I closed my eyes and tried to keep from snapping. I didn't succeed.

"*Vaffanculo,* Jimmy! Did you ever stop to think that maybe *you* caused Lila's injury? If you weren't jumping up and down, taunting that Piney, maybe the guy wouldn't have charged at us. Maybe he would have slowed down or even stopped. Think about it, Jimmy. Maybe you could admit to some fault here, do you think?"

"You bastard." Eve spat the words at me.

"So, what? *You're* the hero?" Jimmy rose to his feet, all 5-foot 4-inches of him. "*You're* the one who grabbed Lila's arm. You pulled her away. That's why she tripped. It's *your* fault!"

"Jimmy, please. Don't do this." Addy's voice was soft, but insistent.

I started to get up, to face off with Jimmy, but Addy touched my shoulder, and I could see tears in her eyes.

"This isn't going to solve anything, Joe," she said.

She was right. I felt my rage subsiding. Maybe women are the best peacemakers. Or maybe Addy just had a way of reaching me.

Jimmy sat down again, too, and Eve gave him a quick hug.

Not all donuts come out with a hole, my Momma would say. Yeah, so we're not all the same, but I couldn't get rid of my distaste for both of them. A few moments passed, each of us dealing with our own thoughts, our anger or resentment or even self-pity. I needed that time to stop seeing red. What the hell was I doing stuck in the woods with this group?

"Maybe the reason he didn't stop is because ... because of what he had on the back of his tractor." Addy seemed to be thinking out loud.

"What are you talking about?" Jimmy still had an edge to his voice.

She hesitated. "You know. That *thing* that fell off the tractor," Addy said.

"I didn't see anything," Jimmy said.

"What?" Eve looked as appalled as I felt.

Sei orbo! How could he be so blind? "The big slab of meat, Jimmy. The body or animal, whatever the hell it was. You didn't see that?"

Jimmy was visibly taken aback, probably trying to process the thought that he wasn't infallible. "I was on the ground...I just jumped out of the way," he mumbled.

"So, whatever it was, I'm thinking the Piney is going to come back for it," Addy said.

"Yup," I said, "and I'm sure he'll bring his shotgun with him."

"So wait, wait just a minute." Jimmy stood and started pacing back and forth in front of the campfire. "If he had something...something like what you said... some kind of dead body ... and it fell off his tractor, sure, he'll come back for it. So we have to move it further away."

"*What?*" Addy jumped up to face Jimmy. He stopped pacing. "It's pitch black out there. How are you going to see it, let alone move it?"

He bent down next to Eve to grab his survival pouch. "I've got a penlight in here …" His voice trailed off and he shook his head. "Yeah, right. All our electronics are dead."

"Try it, Jimmy." Eve stood and handed the pouch to Jimmy, placing herself between Addy and him. She was really getting possessive with him. At least it looked that way to me.

Addy backed up a few paces, obviously catching on to Eve's attachment. "Why not give it a try, Jimmy?" she said. "What do you we have to lose?"

Jimmy shook his head, but then the oddest look appeared on his face. "Electronics …" I guess he was thinking out loud. "Not electronics – *electrical.*" He unzipped the pouch and brought it up to eye level to get a better look inside.

"What is it, Jimmy?" Eve said. "What are you thinking?"

He laughed and shook his head. "The tractor. Of course. The goddamn old tractor."

"You're losing me, Jimmy," Addy said. "What's going on?"

"Okay. I know you don't want another science lecture," he said.

"You got that right." The words came out before I could stop them.

"Yeah, well, listen up." Jimmy held up his hand,

clasping the small penlight, the kind you could buy at any convenience store. "Okay, here's the grand experiment." He pushed a button on the handle and a thin beam of light shone up into the branches.

"How can that be?" Addy was just as shocked as I was.

"No electronics in this baby!" Jimmy shouted.

Chapter Eleven

At that point, I was convinced the little *cazzone* had totally lost it. But the penlight did work when nothing else seemed to. Before I could ask Jimmy to explain, Addy spoke up.

"What's that up there, Jimmy?" she said. "I saw something … something strange. Point the light up again."

"What?" he said with a sneer. "Did you see the Jersey Devil sitting in the branches?" He pointed the light in Addy's face, making her wince and put up a hand to block it.

"Please, Jimmy. There's something up there. On the overhead wires."

After a beat – Jimmy never did respond quickly to anyone's request – he shone the light at the trees again, and we all stared at a monkey-faced barn owl, perched on the telephone wires. The owl didn't look at all upset. It swiveled its head in that creepy way. You know, like that girl in *The Exorcist*.

Addy was still blinking to get her night vision back.

"What a strange creature," she said.

"It's kind of cute," Eve said. The smile on her face was a pleasant change from her usual scowl.

Jimmy seemed to be looking at something else, talking to himself. "The wires. I never noticed them. How could I have missed the wires?" He moved the thin beam of light away from the owl and drew it along the electrical lines that laced through the branches. He stopped when the light reached a utility pole near the back of our broken-down van, murmuring something I couldn't catch.

"What do you understand, Jimmy?" Eve asked. "You said something about understanding."

"Understand? Ha! No, I said Kazakhstan!" He let out a snort. "The Soviet Project K nuclear tests." He was jumping around like a frog on a hotplate, his penlight beam swinging up and down.

"Slow down, Jimmy," Eve said. "Tell us what you're thinking." That seemed to reach him. He shut off the penlight and sat down next to Eve again.

"Okay. So. Just like our Project Starfish Prime, the Soviets also experimented with EMPs in the '60s. You know, electromagnetic pulses. Their Project K in Kazakhstan – get it, that's what the 'K' stands for – was more extensive. And the pulses did more damage."

"So, what's Kazakhstan have to do with us…and the power lines?" I asked.

"Patience, Grasshopper!"

So Jimmy was a fan of the old *Kung Fu* TV series. I wondered which role he pictured himself in – the wise old sage? Yeah, right.

He paused, maybe to collect his thoughts, or more likely to be sure he had our rapt attention. "In one of these Project K tests, the Soviets set off a nuke that sent an electromagnetic pulse down a long telephone line. And I do mean long – like hundreds of miles or something. I guess there's a lot of empty land in Kazakhstan. Anyhow, the telephone line had the usual ceramic insulators and voltage protectors, but that massive EMP fused the lines and blew out the protectors. It was so strong that some sections of wire snapped and fell to the ground – and that's over a hundred miles away."

I was trying to take this all in. Other than working on the 12-volt system in my old truck, I didn't know a thing about electrical pulses, and I certainly didn't have a clue about nukes and EMPs.

"So you mean …" Addy's voice trailed off and she nibbled at her lower lip. She looked like she was doing the times tables in her head. "You mean, the electromagnetic pulse, the pulse that killed our electronics, traveled down these wires and … and because the van was stopped next to a pole, well, we got the brunt of it. Is that it?"

"Bingo!" Jimmy jumped up again and started pacing back and forth.

"But the flashlight, Jimmy. You said something about no electronics before." Eve's voice was soft, like she was trying to draw out a child without getting them all fired up again.

"That's just it," he said. "This little penlight has no microchips. It's just a couple of AA batteries and a light bulb. It also wasn't 'on' when the EMP came through. That matters. Our phones and the van were all turned on, and they're loaded with microprocessors. They can't take a strong EMP."

"Unlike an old Ford tractor," Addy said.

"Yes!" Jimmy seemed jubilant.

I turned to Addy. "How do you know it was a Ford?"

She smiled at me. "I told you about my childhood. We always had farm festivals in the summer back home in Virginia, and some old-timers would show off their restored Ford 8N tractors. That's about as basic a machine as you could imagine."

"And it sure as hell has no microchips," Jimmy added.

It was starting to sink in. "So, we've got a working flashlight. And the Piney has an old Ford tractor that obviously works pretty damned well." I took a breath. "Mystery solved, I guess. But we still don't know how all this happened. Or why." I ran my hands through my hair, trying to see the point of all this. "And it doesn't exactly help our situation here."

"We can see things now," Eve said. I think she would've stuck up for Jimmy no matter what he said.

That tiny flashlight was probably good to have, but we had plenty of bigger problems. "We still have a very pissed-off Piney out there with a shotgun," I said.

Addy peered up the road into the darkness, then turned to me. "How did this...this battle with the Piney start? I mean, when we were exploring, back by that fire road, was the guy shooting at us, or did he shoot...the thing that was tied to the back of his tractor?"

"I don't know, Addy. But whatever's lying in the road out there, I'm sure he wants it back."

Jimmy turned on his penlight again and directed the tiny beam into the darkness, waving it back and forth as if that would help him see better. "So, we've got to go get it before he comes back."

Addy had about as much patience for Jimmy as I did. "Are you out of your mind?" she said.

Eve sprang to Jimmy's defense. "Don't talk to Jimmy that way. He's just trying to do what's best for all of us."

Jimmy put on his best school teacher impersonation. "Okay, let's consider the possibilities. Say he shot someone, and there's a body lying out there. Do you think he wants to abandon that evidence? Or maybe he shot some animal, and that's his dinner that dropped onto the road. Either way, he's going to come back and get it."

"So, let him!" I said.

Jimmy peered up the road again, pointing the feeble penlight beam into the night. "We've either got to drag his 'package' further up the road so it's farther away from us ... he can't be happy about Eve shooting at him, no offense, honey ... or we drag it into the woods so he won't be able to find it until daylight."

Neil MacNeill

Chapter Twelve

If you haven't camped overnight in the woods, you'd be surprised how noisy it gets. Sure, there are no traffic sounds or the familiar hum of your refrigerator, like at home, but there are lots of animal noises. In the Pines, whippoorwills sing all night. It seemed late in the season, but nobody told them that. The tree frogs that can drive you nuts with their constant mee-bee, mee-bee, mee-bee also joined the nighttime chorus.

Against my better judgment, we'd eventually agreed to walk up the road to investigate. It was Eve's idea that Jimmy and I go together, while she and Addy stayed behind with Lila. She probably realized Jimmy would never give up his precious penlight. And maybe she thought Jimmy and I could work out our differences. I had nothing to say to that *cazzone*. I mean, I had a hell of a lot to say, but I decided to keep my mouth shut. Before we set off, though, I pulled Addy aside and asked her to keep a close watch on Eve. I didn't want to get shot by Miss Trigger-Happy when we came walking back.

It wasn't raining as we walked into the darkness, but

there was a heavy mist hanging in the trees that muffled our footsteps. And it was cold for October. I was starting to miss the jacket I'd wrapped around Lila. Every now and then I heard water plopping into a pond or swamp in the woods, and the sounds of some nocturnal creatures searching for their next meal. I was imagining all sorts of things hiding in the Pines on either side of that narrow road.

There was no moon out that night, and if there had been, it would have been hidden by the clouds and mist. The only light we had was the thin beam from Jimmy's penlight, bouncing up and down in front of us, barely cutting through the darkness.

"Can't you keep that damn light still?" Everything Jimmy did got on my nerves.

He just grunted, and we kept on walking. How far ahead had the Piney dropped that thing? It couldn't have been a quarter-mile. But in the darkness, I had no sense of distance. I was just getting accustomed to all the sounds in the woods when I heard the yip of a coyote off to our right.

"What was that?" Jimmy couldn't hide the tremor in his voice.

"A coyote."

"You're kidding me. A coyote? In New Jersey? I thought they were only out west."

We both stopped walking. "You've really led a sheltered life, haven't you, Jimmy? They're all over, even in New Jersey. Haven't you seen one in your neighborhood? They usually come out at night."

In the glow from his penlight, I could see him shaking

his head.

"They don't attack, do they?"

So Jimmy had some chinks in his armor. I decided to have fun with that. "Not *usually*. They go after small animals or sometimes big animals that are hurt or wounded." I couldn't resist adding, "There *have* been cases of coyotes attacking people ..."

His face was hidden in the shadows and I waited for him to respond – nothing. Maybe he caught on to my game, or maybe he decided he'd heard enough about coyotes. We started to walk again. I was beginning to think we should go back to the women and our campfire. What were we going to do when we found the Piney's "package" anyhow? All of Jimmy's suggestions seemed crazy.

"How far up the road *is* this thing?" Jimmy turned to me just as I stopped in my tracks. His light was still shining ahead of us ... straight into the fiery glow of a coyote's eyes. It was standing in the middle of the road, bits of bloody flesh hanging from its mouth. I was so caught off guard, I didn't see the carcass at first. It was half-covered by a ripped-up tarp. A trail of blood glistened on the pavement.

Jimmy finally looked forward and froze. "Jesus Christ!"

I was already backtracking, trying to put some distance between me and the coyote. The damned thing looked right at us and snarled, its head low and ears flattened. I could see the hackles on its back as it clamped its jaw on the dead animal. If that wasn't bad enough, the yips and howls of other coyotes were getting closer.

I'd always thought coyotes hunted alone, not in packs. But if the approaching animals were its pups, momma was sure as hell going to protect them. "We gotta get out of here, Jimmy. But slowly."

He spoke between clenched teeth. "You brought us out here for a goddamned dead deer? And now a coyote's ready to attack us!"

I replied in a hoarse whisper. "*You* were the one who said we had to do this. I didn't know *what* fell off the tractor. I thought it was a big piece of meat, like a dead body."

"You call a body a piece of meat?" Jimmy was breathing hard, glancing behind us for a quick escape.

"Don't turn around, Jimmy. The coyote will see that as a sign of weakness."

"Are you making all this stuff up? From your 'Scout days'?

"You gotta trust me on this, *boombots*. Just keep looking at it and walking backwards. Slowly."

Jimmy spit on the ground. "Right. Sure. Whatever you say."

We both started moonwalking backwards while Jimmy kept the light on the feral beast. "I can't believe I thought we'd find a dead man, and here it's just a deer. A goddamned dead deer."

"Look, that doesn't matter now. But that Piney is surely coming back for his venison steak. If the coyotes don't finish it off first."

It might have been my tunnel vision, the adrenaline, and the blood pounding in my ears, or it could have been all the noises in the woods, but I didn't hear the low rumble of the tractor up the road, and I sure as hell didn't see him approaching us. This time, his headlight was off. And he must have been using Jimmy's bobbing penlight to line up his shot.

Neil MacNeill

Chapter Thirteen

The blast from the shotgun was deafening. In the beam of the penlight, I saw the coyote drop like a rag doll.

"I'm hit! I'm hit!" Jimmy yelled as he pressed his hand against his hip. He focused the penlight there, and I saw two pellet-sized holes near the front pocket of his jeans.

"Can you walk? Jimmy! Are you okay?" I moved closer and put an arm around his waist. "Come on! We gotta get out of here."

He was moaning now, and I could feel his body growing limp. "Come on, Jimmy! You can do this. Move!" As small as he was, he felt like a sack of cement as I hustled him along. I didn't know how badly he was hurt, but I knew we couldn't stick around waiting for another shot from the Piney. "Shut off the damned light! We're a target out here."

He must have heard me because it got real dark, and I felt a little less exposed. I half lifted, half dragged him down the road. I could smell my sweat and feel the pounding of my heart in my ears. The faint glow of our campfire seemed a million miles away. I heard Eve and Addy yelling, but I concentrated all my strength on getting Jimmy back to our base.

In the middle of this chaos, I heard the tractor rev up, its low rumble rising in pitch. A shaft of light swung past as the Piney turned his tractor around, and I realized he probably wasn't going to shoot at us again. That gave me some relief, but only just a little. Jimmy was conscious. I heard him moaning. He was dragging his feet like a zombie. As I lugged him back toward our camp, I yelled to Addy and Eve. "Don't shoot! Don't shoot us!" My voice sounded weak to me, and I hoped they got the message.

When we got closer, I could see Eve with her gun and Addy standing close by. The noise from the tractor receded into the night. We were safe, for now.

"What happened?" Eve screamed at me. "Is Jimmy alright?"

"Help me set him down by the campfire." I gasped, trying to catch my breath. Addy came over and grabbed Jimmy's other arm, and we lowered him to the ground. Eve still had the gun in her hand, staring out into the distance. "Come on, Eve. Put the damn gun away. The Piney is gone now. At least he went the other way."

She seemed to come to her senses, and put the gun back in her purse as she knelt next to Jimmy. He was still holding a hand over his left hip. "Jimmy, honey, you're going to be okay. I'll take care of you," Eve said.

Addy was more direct. "Where are you hit, Jimmy? We've got to take a look at the wound."

He was conscious enough to be embarrassed by that. Even in the dim firelight I saw the color rise in his cheeks. "Here," he whispered, pointing. "My left side."

I stood up and let the two women, kneeling on either side of him, tend to his wounds. I was surprised not to see a blood stain on his jeans.

Addy took the lead. She was the more level-headed of the two. "Okay, Jimmy, I'm going to undo your belt and unzip your pants."

That little *stronzino* squeaked his protest. "Do you have to?"

"It's okay, honey." Eve patted his right hand. "We'll keep your privates covered." She suppressed a giggle.

"It's not funny!" Jimmy sounded more and more like a petulant child.

I had to weigh in. "Look, Jimmy. You've got some buckshot in your side. We've got to ... see how bad it is."

He shook his head in denial, but then closed his eyes and murmured, "Do what you have to."

Addy hesitated just a moment. I saw her hands reach out and then pull back. She rose on her knees to get in a better position, then unbuckled his belt, and with a swift motion, unzipped his fly. I guess she wanted to be clear there was nothing sexual going on. "Eve," she said, "we've got to lift up his hips so we can slide his pants down. Help me."

Now it was Eve's turn to blush. "Okay."

With Addy on one side and Eve on the other, they slid their hands under Jimmy's rear end. "On the count of three," Addy said. "One ... two ... three – lift!"

Jimmy moaned as they raised his hips off the

pavement and nudged down his pants. I know I shouldn't have, but I lost it. "Nice undies, Jimmy." If I was drinking a beer, it would have come out my nose just then. He was wearing red-and-black polka-dot boxers. Eve started giggling again, too.

"Stop it, you guys." Jimmy couldn't have been hurt too badly. His embarrassment was obviously greater than his pain.

"Wait a minute." Addy seemed immune to our laughter. "There's no blood."

"Huh. You're right," Eve said.

Addy took a deep breath and let it out slowly. "Jimmy. Listen to me. Put your hand over your…your genitals." Eve's giggles got louder, but Addy ignored her. "I'm going to pull down your boxers." Eve got up and walked away, snorting in a most unfeminine way. I couldn't blame her. I was having a hard time keeping it in myself.

"Okay, here I go." Addy was slow and gentle in her movements, lifting and pulling Jimmy's boxers away from his wound. She edged down the waistband on his left side … lower and lower … still no blood or gunshot wound. But an odd rectangular bruise was starting to bloom. "What the heck happened here?" Addy said. "Jimmy. What's in your pocket? Your left front pocket?"

Jimmy's eyes went wide as he moved his hand to his pocket, now scrunched down by his hips. "My…my survival tool."

"*Merda!*" I burst out. "Your survival tool literally saved your ass, Jimmy!"

Chapter Fourteen

"What's all the fuss about, Joseph?" I turned to see Lila, half sitting up on her elbows, her eyes blinking away the disorientation and drowsiness. "I thought I heard a gun. Did I dream it?"

"No, you sure as hell didn't dream it." I walked over and crouched down beside her. "How are you feeling?"

"I feel kind of numb, but I guess that's from the drugs. The pain is still there, but it's like it's far away." She glanced over at Jimmy on the ground by the fire, Eve and Addy standing over him. "But what's going on? I'm sure I heard a gun. And why is Jimmy on the ground...with his pants down?"

I had to laugh. It took me a moment to figure out where to begin. A lot had happened while Lila was in la-la land. "You missed a bunch of stuff. When the Piney crashed through our campfire...well, you remember that, right? That's when the log hit your leg and you fell. Then Eve pulled out her gun and shot at the Piney, and there was this big ... 'thing' ... that fell off his tractor."

"I'm sorry, Joseph, but you're not being very clear."

"Okay, you *do* remember Eve doing her best Linda Hamilton impression from 'The Terminator,' right?" I pantomimed the action with my hands. "You know, shooter's stance…both hands on the gun…bang!"

Eve marched over and stood above us, waving her arms. I'd never seen her this agitated. "No, no, no you don't, Joe. You're not the one to tell Lila about all of this. I don't trust you to get it right … to tell her the truth about … all this." She spread her arms to take in the broken-down bus, Jimmy still on the ground, and the deep darkness all around us.

I let out a huff and reared up. "So, you've got it all sorted out, eh? You know the truth and I don't? Well, go ahead, Eve, *you* tell Lila what she missed. Just don't leave out the part you played with your .32 automatic."

Before she could spit out a response, I tramped over and stood next to Addy. She had become my best ally – the only one other than maybe Lila I could trust. My confrontation with Eve had me seeing red. And looking down at Jimmy playing the victim, well, I had no time for him, either. "Pull up your damned pants, Jimmy."

Addy laid a hand on my forearm. "Calm down," she whispered. My muscles tensed for a moment, but then I let out a breath and tried to relax.

"Yeah, you're right. I shouldn't let things get to me like this. I'm just tired of all the drama." Jimmy was still on the ground, staring up at us. He hadn't moved. I tried again. "You're good, Jimmy," I told him. "Some stray buckshot put a few holes in your jeans, not in your hide."

Jimmy still had a wide-eyed look. "But he shot me," he said in a small voice. "The Piney. He shot me."

I should've pitied him right about then, but I just couldn't get to that place. "Come on, Jimmy." Nothing. "Get your ass up!" I reached down to him and tried to soften my voice again. I probably didn't succeed. "You're okay. Just a bruise on your hip. No biggy." Pause. "Here, let me help you up." I waved my hand in front of his face. He stared at me as if I had Covid or something. Finally, he grabbed hold with one hand while pulling up his trousers with the other – not a very smooth move. I yanked him up, maybe harder than I intended, but then again, maybe not. He wobbled like a drunk before steadying himself with Addy's help.

He brushed off his pants, looking embarrassed, but then stopped and craned his neck to take a closer look at the holes in his front pocket. It was pretty hard to see much in the firelight.

"Goddamn it. The fucking Piney shot me!" He looked at Addy and me for sympathy. He sure as hell wasn't going to get any from me.

"The Piney shot the coyote, Jimmy. Not you." I tried to keep my voice level and deal with his delusions. "You just caught some stray buckshot."

"No! No, Joe, that's not the way it happened at all." Jimmy was getting riled up again. "He shot the coyote all right, but he was aiming for me. That's why he took that second shot." Jimmy looked at Addy for support. "You heard the gunshots, Addy, right?"

She glanced at me for a moment, then looked down at the ground. I couldn't tell what she was thinking, but I was sure she wanted to defuse the situation. "Sure, Jimmy. I heard a gunshot."

"No. Not *a* gunshot. He shot *twice* – once at the coyote and once at me. It was probably a double-barreled shotgun. He let loose with both barrels. I know he did."

I threw up my hands. "If that Piney really wanted to shoot you, you'd be dead on the road right now, just like that coyote."

"That's not true, Joe. You were there. You saw it. He hit the coyote, and then he took aim at me, but he missed…just barely missed me." Jimmy fingered the holes in his jeans again.

Eve left Lila's side and stomped over to the three of us. Here we go, I thought. She glared at me but directed her question to Jimmy. "What's Joe saying?"

"The gunshots. Eve, back me up on this. The guy fired twice. The Piney." Jimmy was all red in the face. "He shot the coyote and then he tried to shoot me."

Eve shook her head. For a moment, I thought she'd try to convince Jimmy he was wrong. Maybe the bond between those two was strong enough now that she could make him come to his senses. Yeah, fat chance.

"You were there, Jimmy," she said. "It happened to *you*. Whatever you say, I believe you."

I turned my head and spat on the ground. "Listen, I was there too." I tried to keep the venom out of my voice. "He shot once … the Piney shot once and killed the coyote. Just one shot. And Jimmy happened to be in the way."

Jimmy shook his fists at me. "You liar! Why are you always trying to undermine everything I say?"

As usual, Addy stepped between us and spoke softly

to Jimmy. "No one's undermining you." She glanced over at me, like she wanted me to say some conciliatory words. I didn't have it in me.

Lila broke the tension. "Come on over here, please, Adelaide. All of you, please," she said. "I can't hear what's going on."

I gave Jimmy a hard look but my words were as much for Eve. "Yeah, let's ask Lila what she heard. How many gunshots *she* heard being fired."

Even in the flickering firelight I could see Eve's shoulders stiffen. "So, what? We're going to take the word of that drugged-up woman over Jimmy's? Is that it?"

Lila struggled to get up, pushing against the jump seat for support. Her next words had an edge like I'd never heard from her. "Why don't you just say, 'that drugged up *Black* woman,' Evelyn?" She spoke between clenched teeth. "That's what you're thinking, isn't it?"

"No, Lila. I didn't mean that." If it wasn't so dark, I'm sure I would have seen how mortified Eve looked right then, trying to back-pedal way too late. "That's not what I was trying to say."

Lila's hands clutched the jump seat for support as she steadied herself. "It's always just under the surface. Isn't it, *Eve?*" she said.

No one said anything after that. The chirrs of the crickets and croaks of the frogs, and all the complaints of the night creatures just outside our circle of light grew louder. But now those sounds were punctuated by loud hissing. The smell of damp wool socks entered my nostrils, and I realized the heavy overcast skies were letting loose. It was raining and our carefully made campfire was in danger.

"Jimmy, help me build up the fire so the rain doesn't put it out."

"Like hell I'm going to help you!" Jimmy shot back at me.

"It's for *all* of us! You gonna bite off your nose to spite your face?"

He grabbed Eve's arm and the two of them scrambled to the van's side door, ducking between raindrops.

I banged a palm to my forehead. *Cretino*!

"Addy, please help Lila into the van. I'm going to see if I can keep the fire going."

"Sure, Joe. Of course." She put an arm out to support Lila.

I dragged a few more dead branches onto the smoldering fire in hopes that the flames would outlast the rain. I looked up to try to gauge how bad it was going to get, and was rewarded by a pine-scented raindrop in my eye. "Give me strength," I said under my breath.

I saw no reason to get drenched, so I joined Addy as she was helping Lila up into the van. The rain didn't cool down the tensions between us, though. As Lila hobbled to take a seat, she passed Jimmy and Eve huddled close together, not making eye contact with her. "So," she said in a stage whisper, "you want me to take a seat in the *back* of the bus. Is that it?"

Chapter Fifteen

In my hometown, all the kids went to the same four-room elementary school, and all the families went to the July 4th fireworks festival and the nearby 4-H fairs in the summer. But as small as my rural hometown was, there were distinct ethnic neighborhoods. Of course we lived in the Italian-American section. The other side of town was mostly German and Polish. And down Maple Avenue, there were a bunch of African-American families – the Grahams, Walkers and Johnsons. I was 16 years old when Bobby Johnson died.

My cousin Tony and I were invited to our first deer drive that year. Momma protested, but Poppa and Grandpop overruled her. The deer drive was just down the road from our home in a square-mile plot of woods. I don't think we had our hunting licenses yet, but that didn't seem to matter.

So, Tony and I were at the end of this line of five hunters, spread out on Burgess Road. The "drivers" were about a mile away through the woods on Leeds Road – it ran parallel to Burgess. It was a chilly

November morning, and the guys were passing around a flask. Some were smoking, their shotguns broken over their shoulders. They only entrusted Tony and me with .22 rifles. Tony's dad, Uncle Phil, was alongside him, Mr. Kowalski was next, and then Bobby Johnson.

I heard the crackle of a walkie-talkie, and then the far-off sound of air horns, barking dogs and men shouting. The drive had begun. The whiskey flasks were put away, the cigarettes snubbed out, rifles cocked and brought to the ready. We all waited in silence, peering into the woods to see when a buck would come out in front of us. Deer drives are illegal in New Jersey now, but that was the way hunting was done in my hometown back then. I didn't know any better.

I saw the young buck first – a 4-pointer, just walking toward us through the trees. I raised my rifle but hesitated. Tony took that as his cue. He stepped forward, out of line, to get a better bead on the deer, who froze when he caught wind of us. I don't know why, but Tony stepped forward again. I guess he wanted to make sure he got the deer. I held my breath, waiting for the shot. Another deer, a doe, came crashing through the pines, and in its panic ran into the buck. Someone shouted. I'm not sure how it all happened, but Bobby Johnson swung his shotgun toward the deer and fired.

The shot went wild, and the doe ran back into the woods. He maimed the buck, though. It went down on its front legs. Someone, I think maybe Mr. Kowalski, rushed forward and finished him off. But one of the buckshot pellets got Tony. He went down on his knees, screaming in pain, holding his hands to his face. Uncle

Phil bent down next to his son and yelled for an ambulance. He pulled a bandana from his pocket and pressed it over Tony's right eye.

Our nearest hospital was a good 15 miles away, and a couple of the hunters were our local ambulance drivers, so that wasn't an option. Mr. Kowalski ran to his pickup, parked nearby, and raced up. Uncle Phil cradled Tony in his arms and got in the truck. They sped away.

Tony lost most of the sight in his right eye. That changed his life forever, but he seemed to get past it. Instead of going to college, he took a job in a local glass factory for a while. Of course, he couldn't drive at night.

Tony never blamed Bobby Johnson, and some of the hunters tried to console Bobby, but others said horrible things behind his back. He couldn't walk into town without people either staring at him or looking the other way. I couldn't believe how people who'd been standing right next to him, sharing their whiskey flasks, fellow hunters out on a crisp fall morning, could turn on him. Like Lila said, sometimes it's just below the surface.

Everything spiraled out of control for Bobby. He started drinking too much. I guess he couldn't deal with the guilt. A few weeks later, he put a gun in his mouth and blew his brains out. He was 22 years old.

Addy *did* take Lila to the back of the van. It was the only place with a bench seat where she could elevate Lila's injured leg. She made sure Lila was as comfortable as possible, then settled into a seat in front of her. I stood in the aisle, trying to figure out what to do next. Addy glanced over at me, but it was so dark in the van, I couldn't read her face. I guess I should have joined her in that narrow seat – like Jimmy and Eve had done. Who could fault them for wanting some human companionship? Hell, for all we knew, the whole world had stopped.

Instead, I sat down across the aisle from Addy. Shut off from the chaos and darkness, enclosed in our glass and metal cocoon, I guess everyone else felt safe, but I couldn't get comfortable. I was too wound up.

The rain came down hard for a while, but it didn't last. The van's windows fogged up, and the chilly night air was getting harder to ignore. It grew quiet. We were all exhausted. Everyone seemed to drift off, but I couldn't sleep. I decided to step outside again and try to revive the fire.

I was relieved to see a few glowing embers, so I bent down and blew on them to get things going again. Some small branches under the jump seat had escaped much of the rain. After breaking them into smaller pieces, I fed them into the fire one at a time. There was more smoke than flame at first, and my eyes started to water. Eventually I heard the welcome snap of twigs and branches drying out and catching fire.

I raised one corner of the jump seat and brushed off the rest of the water as best I could before sitting down. Everything was so damp, and I was pretty wet too, so it didn't seem to matter. I suddenly felt all alone in the universe. For the first time since our world stopped, I thought about my daughter in Ohio. Was she experiencing the same thing? Were her neighbors helping her, or fighting with her for what they thought were the last pieces of civilization? I had no idea how widespread this whole thing was. With all the electronic devices knocked out, I was feeling pretty hopeless.

Lost in thought, I didn't hear Addy come up until she was standing by my side, rubbing her hands over her shoulders. At first, I thought she was cold. "Is everything okay?" I asked. I let out a sharp laugh as I realized how asinine that question was – *nothing* was okay.

"I couldn't stand it in there anymore," she said.

"What do you mean?"

"It's Jimmy and Eve." She waited a beat before continuing. "They're touching each other."

I didn't get it at first. Maybe I was naïve or just the thought of the two of them romantically involved, if that's what you called it, seemed ridiculous. "You mean, like, *touching* each other?"

Now it was Addy's turn to laugh. "Yeah! They're really going at it … you know, moaning and stuff. I'm surprised Lila didn't wake up."

"*Che cazzo!* Is he … is Jimmy molesting her?"

"No. It seemed pretty consensual to me," Addy said. "They didn't even slow down when I walked past them."

We both fell silent and let the crackling campfire and the sounds of all the night creatures around us have their say. Nature! I guess it was any port in the storm for those two. I kept trying to make sense of it, and didn't realize I spoke my next words out loud. "He's easily in his 40s or 50s, and she's practically jailbait."

"I don't know that term," Addy said. "Jailbait?"

"Sorry. Um, really? It's not a very nice thing to say." I tried to apply some kind of PC filter. "It's a girl who's underage, you know, for sex. But she looks older, and she's very hot…and this isn't coming out well, is it?"

Addy shook her head but then reached out and put a hand on my shoulder. "It's okay, Joe, I get it. My Mom would have washed my mouth out with soap if I talked like that, but I get it."

I laid my hand across hers and for a moment I felt a little spark. Our brief interlude came to an end when Addy let out a shout and ripped her hand away.

"Look! Up the road – the lights!"

I got up, and we rushed around the campfire to get a better view. Dazzling balls of light danced in the woods ahead of us. They formed and dissipated, like someone putting on a crazy light show. For a moment I thought it was the Piney and his tractor, but this was a different kind of light. It was shimmering, blue-green, as if a magician were setting off explosive powder, with clouds of mist that caught fire. The light flashes moved back and forth, but didn't seem to be getting any closer. The Pines grew silent, and I heard a strange popping sound. Addy started to move toward the lights.

I grabbed her arm, and a wave of déjà vu washed over me as I realized I'd gone through the same motions with Lila earlier that evening. Addy's muscles tensed. She yanked her arm away and started walking up the road toward the lights. She raised her arms to the sky and called out to the shape-shifting clouds of light. "Take me! I'm ready!" There was a loud pop and then it went dark.

It's like I blinked and everything I'd seen was just a fading movie inside my head. With the return of darkness, the sound of frogs and crickets resumed. It was as if nothing at all had happened.

"What did she think that was, Joseph? The Rapture?"

My head whipped back and forth between Addy in a dead faint on the side of the road, and Lila shaking her head, leaning on the van for support.

"When did you get here ... did you see...?" I couldn't process it all.

"Don't worry about me," Lila said. "Go take care of your lady friend. You'll have to explain to her that she hasn't ascended to the Pearly Gates."

I ran over to Addy, knelt down and put my hand under her head. In the shifting shadows of light from our fire, her face looked flush, her cheeks wet with tears. She opened her eyes but still had a faraway, unfocused look.

"Addy. Addy, are you hurt?"

She blinked and seemed to come out of a trance. "This isn't heaven, is it?" she whispered.

"No. No ... this is more like hell."

She shook her head.

"Did you really think it was ...?" I asked.

She wrinkled her nose, and took a moment to answer. "The End Times? Yes, I guess I did."

"I had no idea you were so religious."

"Think about it, Joe. The whole world stops. The plane crash. Even the Piney attacking us. And those lights. They were so ... heavenly."

I looked up at the dark branches above us, reaching

into the low-hanging clouds. I didn't want to insult her beliefs, but I couldn't get my head around what she was saying. "I don't understand how...I'm just not inclined in that direction."

She stared at me. "So, you're not saved?"

I forced a laugh, trying to make light of her question. "Not lately." I waited for her to say something more, maybe to start proselytizing. I'm glad she didn't. She murmured something that sounded like "sorry for you," but maybe I didn't hear her right.

"Come on, let me help you up and check you out. I mean, make sure you're okay." I stood and helped her to her feet. She brushed off her pants and then took my hand as we walked back to the campfire. Lila was sitting on the jump seat, staring off into space. Jimmy and Eve, looking awkward and sheepish, were warming their hands by the fire.

I kept my distance, and tried not to imagine the two of them getting it on. That all went out the window when I noticed Eve's blouse had Tuesday's buttons in Wednesday's holes. *Merda*!

Addy let go of my hand and walked right up to them. "Did you see the light?" she asked. At first I thought it was a spiritual question.

"There've been hundreds of UAP sightings in South Jersey," Jimmy said. "That's the new term, you know – Unexplained Aerial Phenomena ..."

"Swamp gas," Eve cut in.

Jimmy gave her a puzzled look. "Ha! That's what the government wants you to believe. They've been saying it's reflections from the planet Venus and things like swamp gas ever since the Roswell incident in 1947."

Eve didn't acquiesce this time. "No, Jimmy. That was a perfect example of swamp gas."

"How could that be?" Addy asked. "I mean, it was so luminous, so beautiful. It was truly otherworldly."

"Look, we're in an area with lots of marshes and swamps – stagnant water," Eve explained. "All the dead organic matter that ends up in the marshes eventually decays. When it does, it produces methane. And when the swamp is disturbed by, say, an animal like a deer…"

"Or a coyote," I butted in.

Eve gave me a look but then continued. "As I was saying, an animal walking through the swamp disturbs the sediment. The methane mixes with phosphines and bubbles to the surface. When it does, oxygen in our atmosphere makes it burst into flame."

We were all silent after all that scientific babble. Then Lila said, "You really are a plant biologist, aren't you, Evelyn." I couldn't tell if she was praising Eve or being sarcastic.

"I'm a microbial biologist," Eve corrected.

"Not to mention a sharpshooter." I couldn't resist the dig. She ignored me.

"But I had a really good bio-chem prof in school. That's where I learned about swamp gas. He even did this little experiment in class. He released a small amount of methane and phosphine, and they ignited spontaneously. It was pretty cool."

"Wait a minute." Jimmy never let things go. "You said the swamp had to be disturbed for the gas to bubble up to the surface and ignite."

"That's right," Eve said. "It only ignites when it hits the atmosphere."

"So, what…or who…disturbed the swamp up the road?" He looked around, waiting for one of us to take the bait.

Lila spoke up. "James, you're not suggesting the Piney was behind all this, are you?"

"Why not!" Jimmy threw his hands up. He must have been one crazy teacher. "You *know* he's out there…somewhere. You *know* he has it in for us."

I couldn't take it anymore. "No, Jimmy, we have no idea if he has it in for us or not. Did you ever stop to think that maybe *we're* the problem?"

"What the hell are you talking about, Joe?"

Addy tried to defuse the argument. "We really don't know his motives," she said. "He could just be trying to protect his domain."

"Ha! You're both delusional!" Jimmy paced back and forth between the van and the campfire. "He's some kind of recluse. A hermit. He sees us here, and what's he do? First he shoots at you two, then he crashes his tractor through our campfire. And then…then he comes back and shoots at me."

"Oh, not again." I gave up on the conversation, and stomped around the van, into the shadows.

I was back there mumbling to myself and kicking at stones, when I realized I really needed to pee. Nothing like taking a piss out in the country – like the Elton John song, you know? As I finished and zipped up, a movement in the darkness caught my eye. That's when I saw the beam of a flashlight in the woods.

Chapter Sixteen

There's a natural rhythm when people walk – they swing their arms back and forth. If you're walking in the dark with a flashlight in your hand, you resist that movement so the light stays in front of you. But the light will still rise and fall with each step. That's what I saw in the woods. Not a shimmering ball of light like before, but a guy walking through the trees, maybe on one of those fire roads Addy and I had seen before. A guy with a flashlight.

I yelled out to him and ran to alert our group. I guess they were still arguing about Pineys and swamp gas because they didn't pay much attention to me at first. So I screamed at them as I slid to a stop by the campfire. "Look in the woods, *boombots*! There's someone there!"

We crowded together at the edge of the road, looking at the bobbing light. "Holy shit, he's back!" Jimmy muttered.

Ignoring Jimmy's fixation with the Piney, I yelled out. "Yo! You there. In the woods. I'm talking to you!"

"What are you doing?" Eve hissed at me. "What if

he … we don't know what he's up to."

I tried again. "Yo, mister! Come talk to us!"

The light stopped its bobbing motion and then went out. Just like that. I listened hard above the sounds of the Pines, but I didn't hear anyone walking in the woods, and I sure as hell couldn't see any movement.

I glanced over and saw Eve pull the pistol from her handbag. Nudging Addy, who was standing next to me, I whispered. "Here we go again."

"Eve?" Addy's voice was soft, cajoling. "Please put the gun away."

Eve put both hands on the pistol and raised it up like 007, scanning the darkness for danger. "No way. Whoever's out there is not friendly."

"Stand away from the fire!" Jimmy looked back and forth between our campfire and the last place we'd seen the light in the woods. "We're open targets here – backlit against the fire. It'll be too easy for him to pick us off."

"Have you gone totally crazy, James?" Leave it to Lila to put him in his place. But Jimmy ignored her, crouching down and frog-walking along the edge of the road like a grade-school kid playing dodgeball.

Jimmy's paranoia was spiraling out of control. I had to say something. "Come on!" I yelled. "Just because the guy shut off his flashlight doesn't mean he's going to shoot at us."

"Don't you get it, Joe?" Jimmy was still talking in whispers, as if the guy in the woods was listening. "He obviously doesn't want to be seen, and with his light off, he can see us clear as day."

"You and Eve always assume the worst! That's the

way you look at the world, isn't it? 'The bad guys are out there and they're coming to get me.'"

Jimmy shrugged off my comment, but in the shadows from the guttering campfire, I saw Eve's face turn red.

"Yeah, that's right," she spat. "And when the bad guys come, I'm ready for them."

Addy tried again. "They could just be lost, like us. Maybe they see us standing here, arguing with each other, and they don't want to have anything to do with us."

Eve shook her head. "You don't get it. If the guy is armed ..." She took a breath and started over. "Okay, he's out there in the woods, and there's no law and order now that everything's stopped. And even if things were still working, there are no police anywhere around here. For all we know, it's utter chaos everywhere right now. There's nobody to stop him. If he comes for us, he'll take whatever he wants." Her voice rose in pitch, and I saw a shiver run down her body. "Who do you think he's going to rape? He's going to rape the pretty young blonde with big boobs. He's going to rape *me*."

Addy turned away and walked back to the warmth of the campfire. "You poor soul," she murmured.

I tried to talk sense to Eve. "Look, I know you're upset, but...please. Let's wait a bit and see what happens. See if...see if the guy comes forward. We don't know anything about him or what he's doing. Just wait to see what he does next. Maybe we can talk to him."

Jimmy butted in. "You hold on to that gun, Babe." He turned to look at me. "We'll wait alright. But we'll be ready. Eve will be ready with her pistol."

Minutes crawled by as we scanned the darkness for approaching danger. It was getting under my skin. If we were going to be attacked, which I doubted, I wanted to be by Addy. I took her hand, and we walked over to the campfire. Jimmy and Eve, our very own Mulder and Scully, stood shoulder to shoulder, still gazing into the woods for the approaching "bad guys."

Lila let out a loud breath and limped over to the jump seat. "Whoever was out there isn't interested in us," she said, maybe as much to the stranger in the woods as to us. "Let them go. We need to deal with our immediate concerns and get through the night." She took our silence as agreement, so she continued in her best Office Manager tone. "Let's get back to our original plan."

"Always the organizer, aren't you?" Jimmy said.

Lila stared him down. "I'm trying to bring order to the chaos, James. Maybe you can help increase our chances of survival." She was talking his language now.

I'm sure Jimmy said something under his breath, but he nodded in agreement. That was probably as much as we'd get from him.

"Joseph. The fire is dwindling," Lila said. "You and James gather more wood while we still have some light." She didn't wait for either of us to object. "I know it's wet, but stack the branches and twigs next to the fire so they can dry out." She turned to Addy. "The 'women folk' will sort out the rest." Then she waved her arm at Eve. "Come on, Evelyn. Put the gun away and let's try to come up with a plan."

"Yeah, kum-ba-yah," Eve mumbled, but she walked over to join Lila and Addy.

Teaming up with Jimmy to gather wood was the last thing I wanted to do, but in the interests of harmony – ha! – well, I guess for Lila's sake, I decided to do it. We ventured out as far as we had light enough see, to tell a dead branch from a snake in the darkness. Jimmy said he couldn't use his penlight and carry branches at the same time, so we did a lot by feel. We worked in silence. I'm Italian, so that just didn't sit right. Yeah, we talk a lot. Not only that, but I kept thinking about what Eve had said. I decided to broach the subject with her new "boyfriend."

"Do you think Eve was abused or something?"

That stopped Jimmy in his tracks. "Abused? Nah, I don't think so." I could see him smiling in the dim light. "She was coming on to me pretty strong."

Che palle! He sure didn't have any boundaries. "Um, okay," I said. "Maybe I really don't want to talk about it after all. I was just wondering."

We continued our work and eventually made a decent pile of firewood at our "home base." Once we agreed we'd had enough, I arched my back to get the kinks out and looked over at the women. Addy and Eve were huddled around Lila, sitting on the jump seat, deep in conversation. I don't know what it is about women – they find it a lot easier to share their feelings than men do. I walked over. "So, have you solved all our problems?" I asked.

"No, Joseph, we have not." Lila's voice was stern but she had a smile for me. "But we did decide to go back to our original plan – two of us will stay awake and act as lookout, and the others will rest or sleep as best they can," she said.

I scanned their faces to see if everyone agreed to this. "Who's got lookout duty first?" I asked.

"You and me, Joseph."

That took me by surprise. I guess I thought I'd be paired with Addy, and Jimmy with Eve, but then that would leave Lila as the odd one out. Eve also looked uncomfortable, but not for the reason I thought.

"I'll go along with this, but it's not the way I'd do it," she said.

"What's the problem?" I asked.

"I'm the only one with a gun."

I held out my hand. "That's easy. Give me the gun while you rest."

Her lip curled up, and she snarled at me. "No way in hell, big boy!"

Chapter Seventeen

It'd been a good idea to remove the jump seat from the van and position it against the front bumper. It was close enough to our fire for warmth and also gave a view up the road...for whatever we could see in the murky darkness. But there wasn't room for two of us on it. So I stood next to Lila, leaning against the hood. She still had a limp, and standing would probably make it worse. I didn't mind giving up the seat. A lot of my work involved kneeling and crouching, slathering mortar on bricks, or working stone with a mallet and chisel. So standing was pretty much a luxury for me.

Neither one of us spoke for a while, and I started to think about how bad it might be back home. Dark strip malls. Abandoned cars on I-80. Dead gas pumps. And lots of angry people. Jimmy and Eve had planted the seeds of paranoia, and they were starting to grow.

What if the guy in the woods really *did* have it in for us? What if the Piney was an evil son-of-a-bitch, and not the benign hermit I'd imagined? Here we were, like cavemen huddled around a fire, trying to keep the monsters at bay. All I could do was stare into the glowing embers, watching a meager flame appear and then just as quickly disappear.

My stomach growled. I was really missing dinner. I looked down at Lila and saw beads of sweat on her forehead. That didn't make sense in the cool October night. "Are you okay?" I knelt down and took her hand.

She had a vacant stare, and her voice came out in hisses. "I need to eat something."

"Yeah, I'm hungry, too."

"You don't understand." She was shivering. "I'm diabetic … Type 2. It's my blood sugar …"

Madre di Dio! I had no idea. "What can I do? How can I help you?"

"My pocketbook. It's in the van. On the floor by the back seat. I have some chocolate and crackers. Please, Joseph."

I froze for a second. Stuck in the woods with no way to get help, well, I realized this could really be bad.

Getting into the van and shuffling to the back in the flickering firelight was easy enough. But when I got down on my hands and knees to search for the pocketbook, it was just too dark. All I could do was feel around on the floor. Then Addy touched my shoulder, and my heart jumped. "Jesus Christ, you sure know how to sneak up on a guy."

"Don't use the Lord's name in vain," she murmured. She was getting all holy on me after her religious experience with the swamp gas.

I shook my head and tried to calm my breathing. "It's Lila," I said. "She's having some kind of diabetic attack."

"What can we do?"

"Her pocketbook. She said it's down here."

"Does she have an insulin pen or something?"

"No." I was getting frustrated just talking. Lila needed help, and fast. "Chocolate and crackers. Just help me find the damned pocketbook."

We groped around all over, and I was giving up hope.

"Got it!" she said, loud enough to wake the slumbering lovers a few seats up from us. But they didn't stir. I think Addy realized her outburst was too loud, because she leaned in real close and whispered in my ear. "Let me come and help."

Yeah, she was getting to me.

We edged up the aisle and out the door. Lila was hugging herself and swaying back and forth. I didn't know crap about diabetes, but I sure hoped whatever was in her pocketbook would do the trick.

She rummaged through it, tossing out tissues, a change purse and reading glasses until she pulled out a Hershey bar. Her hands shook as she tried to separate the wrapper. It was frustrating to watch her struggle. I wanted to grab it from her and rip it apart with my teeth. But she managed to pull off the wrapping and take a big bite. Addy and I just watched her, hoping this would help even out her blood sugar. She stuffed the rest of the chocolate bar into her pocketbook and pulled out some peanut-butter crackers. Seeing her chew on them made my mouth go dry. "You need water or you'll choke." I took one of the bottles we had stashed next to the jump seat, unscrewed the top and handed it to her.

She took a long swig. The tiniest smile appeared at the corners of her mouth. "Thank you," she said between swallows. "Thank you, Joseph. And Adelaide." Her smile widened. "You saved me."

I shrugged. "Why didn't you tell me you needed to eat? That you had this blood-sugar problem?"

"I don't have enough food to share." She looked down at the ground.

"Oh, you sweet thing," Addy said.

"*Merda*! You've got to look out for Number One. It's every man for himself out here." I glanced at Addy and now I was the one embarrassed. "I mean every person. Jeez. You know what I mean." Addy's expression was soft; there was a smile in her eyes. She was probably amused by my backpedaling. For some reason a pretty uncharitable thought occurred to me and I couldn't help letting it out. "Do you think Jimmy would share if he had some food?"

"That's not very kind," Addy scolded. Like I said, she was acting as my moral watchdog.

Best to change the subject. "So, don't you need some kind of sugar tablets or something?"

"No, Joseph. The chocolate and crackers usually work fine. I'm on medication … for my diabetes. And as long as I have some food every few hours, my blood-sugar levels are fine."

"Yeah, it has been a long time since we've all eaten," I said.

"Would you like one or two crackers?" Lila asked.

I didn't reply. Sure, I was hungry, but taking crackers from Lila at that point seemed like stealing candy from a baby. It just wasn't right.

Addy spoke up. "You need them much more than we do." She looked at me. "We can get by."

My stomach didn't agree, but I nodded.

"You eat as much as you need to stabilize things," Addy said.

"Thank you, Adelaide. I'll have one more cracker now and save the rest for later." She pulled another from the wrapper and took little nibbles on it between sips of water. It looked like she was trying to make it last as long as possible.

I was starting to salivate. "So, you'll be okay now?"

"I think so, Joseph. I mean, it was pretty bad this time, but I should be alright now. I just need a little time." She looked up at me, her voice faint but level. "Everything will be better in the morning. The authorities will sort out this EMP or whatever James called it. I'm confident our governor will get things under control."

"Our governor?" I said. "You think some bureaucrat in Trenton is going to fix this mess? Really?"

"There are lots of competent people in our state government, Joseph, including our governor. You shouldn't be so cynical."

I walked over, grabbed a branch, and threw it on the fire. I was trying to control myself, but I had a history with the State of New Jersey. "You really think the governor is capable of dealing with all this? That hack politician?" She got me started and now I was on a rant. "I've had my run-ins with the state, telling me how I should do my job. 'Always wear a respirator mask.' 'No dry cutting.' 'No dry grinding.' *Merda*! I know when to wet-down stone. I know how to protect myself when I work. I'm part of a long line of Italian masons, going back centuries. Trenton doesn't know shit."

"Joseph, I'm sure you don't know the woman." I could tell Lila was also trying to keep her emotions in check. "The governor's a good person. As you know, I work for the county. I've been in meetings with her. She has good values. And I believe she'll do the right thing."

"I pray she will," Addy said.

Yeah, and fiddle-dee-dee, tomorrow's another day.

Chapter Eighteen

As you might imagine, our conversation didn't go anywhere after that. I guess we all looked at the world differently. I respected Lila. I really did. But she seemed to have a child-like trust in the government. And Addy? Sure, I was attracted to her. But her Bible-thumping was getting on my nerves.

The three of us were quiet for a while. Lila set the water bottle back down and folded her hands on her lap. She still looked weak, drained. And during the lull in our conversation, I could see her nodding off.

I approached Addy. Keeping my voice low, I suggested we help Lila back into the van. Addy and I could stay up and watch for whatever might come down the road.

So it was back to the two of us, keeping the world at bay. Addy was on the jump seat, and since the area around the campfire had pretty much dried out, I sat on the ground next to her. We were kind of close. She could lean into me if she was tired, but we were both wide awake. The way we were sitting, well, her open collar was at eye level for me. I was trying not to stare at her *tette* as we talked, so I ended up looking at her throat and the little silver cross she wore around her neck.

What are the two subjects they always tell you to avoid? Politics and religion, right? Well, fools rush in, and since I'd already aired my opinion about politics, I decided to ask Addy about her faith. "So, were your parents strict about religion and stuff? I mean, did you go to church every Sunday, no exceptions?"

It had been so quiet, I think I might have startled her with that question. Either that or she wanted to give it some thought before responding. "Yes. We're Evangelicals, and our faith is strong. Our whole family down in Virginia was raised in the church – cousins, nieces and nephews. I don't see a lot of that here in Jersey."

"Hmm. Well, there's more, what's the word … diversity here." I kept my eyes forward, so I'm not sure how she reacted to that. "And that's okay, I guess. My Momma used to say, 'We're all God's children.'"

I looked up at her now, and she was smiling. "I like that sentiment, Joe."

A loud snap from the fire caught us off guard, and we both jumped. One of the bigger branches had split and fallen into the embers. I got up and laid another bundle of twigs on top. We'd probably need to gather more wood before daylight. I had no way of telling what time it was – 2 a.m.? Not even midnight?

I sat back down next to Addy.

"And what about you?" she asked.

My mind was somewhere else, so I didn't know what she meant.

"Your upbringing? You more or less said you weren't saved, but it sounds like you were raised in the Catholic faith."

"Oh. Yeah, well, do you know any Italian-Americans who *weren't* raised Catholic?"

"And now?"

I let out a long breath. "Too many things got in the way. The Church has way too much baggage. So, no, I don't go to Mass anymore."

"But don't you believe God has His plans for us?"

"Ha! Yeah, right. He wanted to give us a kick in the ass, so he sent down a divine bolt of lightning and busted all our electronics." I waited for her to respond, but she kept silent. "Short answer: No."

"That's a shame, Joe. You seem like a good person. You care about others. But you don't believe in God's will?" She got up and started pacing between the van and the fire. "You know the verse, right? God moves in mysterious ways."

"Oh, come on, Addy. Do you really believe this electronic Armageddon is part of God's plan?"

She didn't say anything else, but kept walking back and forth, like she was trying to work through a problem or something. Maybe she thought I was ripe for conversion. I don't know, but I wasn't going to go there.

I looked up when she stopped and pointed at a

nearby tree. "What's that vine over there? Hanging from that branch," she said. "It looks like it's moving."

I stood and put my arm around her shoulder. "Don't be upset. That's not a vine. It's a snake."

Addy's shriek ricocheted inside my skull. All I could do was hold her and move my body between the snake and her. She buried her face in my shoulder and kept screaming and screaming. My bear hug couldn't calm her.

In all this commotion, I didn't realize that Jimmy and Eve had emerged from the van. He grabbed one of the branches from the fire and poked at the big black snake. It dropped to the shoulder of the road and coiled up in the sand. I've never seen a snake this big, except maybe in zoos. A strong musky odor mixed with the smoke from the fire. The damn thing hissed and raised itself to strike. Its head was much wider than its body.

Eve yelled, "Stand back!" She raised her pistol and fired off two rounds. My ears rang. Anyone for miles around must have heard that gunshot. The snake was still writhing, but Eve had hit it. Its stench was stronger than ever. Jimmy poked at it again, but it didn't seem to have enough life in it to fight back.

Addy pulled away from me and pointed at it. "Kill it! It's evil. Can't you see? Kill it!"

I closed my eyes and tried to find some place of sanity. "It's already dead, Addy," I said, but I'm not sure she heard me. She kept her arm raised, pointing at the still wiggling snake.

"Go ahead, Jimmy," I said. "Put it out of its misery."

He nudged the snake into the fire. Lila limped over to join us, and we all watched the snake's death throes as its black scales turned to gray.

Neil MacNeill

Chapter Nineteen

"You didn't need to kill it, Evelyn."

"It was attacking Jimmy," Eve responded.

"It was evil." Addy still looked shaken.

Surprisingly, Jimmy didn't join in the argument.

"It was just a snake," I said. "A big mother Black Racer. Still, just a snake."

"No." Eve looked at me. "It was a Black Rat Snake. They're probably the biggest snakes in Jersey. They can grow to over 8 feet."

We all looked at Eve. How the hell did she know so much about snakes?

"My cousin," she said. "The Park Ranger I mentioned? He had pet snakes growing up, and the biggest one was a Black Rat Snake. They're not venomous. They're constrictors."

Whatever the breed of snake, the dead reptile was turning into ashes, its foul odor slowly being replaced with the homey smells of the campfire.

Jimmy broke his silence. "We should have eaten it."

"That's pretty disgusting, James," Lila said.

"It's evil. It needs to burn." Addy was certainly secure in her beliefs. Snakes equal evil.

I tried to add some levity. "I hope it doesn't have any relatives nearby," I said. No one laughed at my joke.

"I'm surprised it was out this late in the season," Eve said. "They're natural climbers, and usually find a hollow in a tree to hibernate."

"I hate snakes," Addy murmured.

I was going to make a joke about Indiana Jones, but I didn't think Addy would appreciate the reference. I glanced over and saw her mouth tight, her arms crossed over her chest. Was her reaction to the snake an irrational fear or was it Biblical, wrapped up in her faith? I didn't want to ask.

Lila still seemed out of it, like she had a bad hangover or something, but she managed to get back into office manager mode. "Okay, people," she said. "Now that this situation is taken care of, let's concentrate on our immediate issues again. We need more firewood."

"You're not suggesting Joe and I go out again, are you?" It was obvious Jimmy wanted nothing to do with me. And the feeling was mutual.

"I am, indeed, James. You and Joseph did a fine job before."

Jimmy hung his head in resignation. I rotated my neck, trying to get out the kinks, and did a little isometric stretch of my arms in my best World Wrestling Federation impression. Hey, a bit of physical intimidation always helps.

"Yeah, okay, Mr. Muscle Man. I get it." He blew out a breath. "Let's get it over with, maybe go back down the road *behind* the van this time."

I had a eureka moment. "Jimmy. Before we go. Do you have some kind of tape in that survival pouch of yours?"

I could see the wheels turning in his head, trying to figure out if I was laying a verbal trap for him.

"Yeah ... some medical tape and gauze," he said. "What of it?"

"It's as dark as the devil's pockets out there. Do you think you could tape that penlight of yours to your wrist? It would sure as hell help us find more branches ... without tripping over snakes."

That got a smile out of him. "Good thinking, MacGyver!" He scurried back into the van, and when he came out again, he waved his left arm around, pointing the beam at the trees, into our eyes and everywhere else in between. I wished he'd had a hat we could tape the light to, but no such luck.

We had no choice but to work together because Jimmy had our improvised "wrist light." Of course, that meant he did most of the pointing – "hey, there's a good-sized log!" – and I did most of the lifting and carrying. I was beginning to regret my earlier pro-wrestler pantomime.

I don't know if there's any scientific evidence for this, but I think Italians can't stand silence. If there's someone else around, even a stranger, they have to talk to them.

And, well, I couldn't resist asking Jimmy about his new love interest. "So. You and Eve are quite an item now."

"What of it?"

"Well. You know. You're so different."

"Is that some kind of racist slur? What, because I'm Asian and she's White?"

"Relax, Jimmy. I mean your age difference."

He stopped walking, and the flashlight beam went still. I heard him take a few breaths. Was he going to go off on me? Instead, he surprised me with a rational thought.

"We're in a bubble out here, Joe. The whole world may have stopped dead. This EMP could set civilization back for years."

"Yeah, the shit's hit the fan. But what's that got to do with…"

"She's very intelligent, Joe." He let that sink in. "And she digs me." Just as I was starting to have some empathy for the guy, he ruined it by saying, "And man, is she hot!"

Merda! "Jimmy, she's just a kid. Have some respect."

He waved his arms around. The flashlight beam danced over the road and the trees. "Don't talk to me about respect," he sneered. "What about you and Addy?"

Now it was my turn to get pissed off. "What about her?"

He let out a grunt. "Oh, come on, Joe. I've seen how you are with her."

My hands balled into fists. "We're simpatico. But that's as far as it goes. What of it?"

Jimmy smirked. "Right. So she hasn't opened up her

legs for you yet?"

"I've had about enough of you, you little prick!" Dumping the firewood, I reached over and grabbed him by his shirt. I might have lifted him off the ground. I don't remember.

"Let go of me, you stupid Dago!" His arms flailed around, the tiny flashlight beam strobing into my eyes.

I threw him to the ground. I probably knocked the wind out of him, but I couldn't see where he landed.

"You Goddamn asswipe! You broke my light!"

Neil MacNeill

Chapter Twenty

I walked back toward "camp" alone. I didn't give a damn if Jimmy was whining in humiliation or even in pain. Let him lick his wounds on the side of the road in the dark. I'd had enough. He could say whatever he wanted about me, but when he insulted Addy, that was different. All I wanted to do was put some distance between me and him. As I made my way back, the light from our campfire silhouetted our lifeless van. It looked like a half-closed eye in the darkness.

When I rejoined the group, Lila must have seen the look on my face. "Okay, Joseph, what's going on … and where's James?" she asked.

"I left him by the side of the road."

Addy came to my side. "What happened, Joe?"

I closed my eyes and gave a quick shake of my head. I didn't want to tell her what Jimmy had said about her. "He disrespected you," I muttered.

She put her hand on my arm and smiled up at me. "Oh, Joe."

But then Eve was in my face. "What the hell did you

do?" She spat out her words, her face bright red in the firelight. "You slugged him, didn't you?"

"He stepped over the line," I told her. "I couldn't take it anymore."

Eve glared up at me.

"I didn't hit him. But I might have thrown him to the ground."

She wouldn't get out of my face. "You had to pick a fight with him, didn't you, you big shit?"

"So, shoot me!" Not the best thing to say, given Eve's close personal relationship with her pistol, but that's what came out. Addy squeezed my arm, and I got the signal – chill.

The silence that followed was broken only by the snaps and hisses from our campfire. I caught some movement by the side of the van, and saw Jimmy hobble into the light, his face smudged, his lips tight. Of course, Eve rushed over and hugged him. I had to turn away.

"I don't know what your plans are for the rest of the night, Lila, but I'm done here," I said.

"You do what you have to, Joseph."

As I stomped over to the van, Addy followed me.

I grabbed a seat in back and tried to get comfortable leaning against a window. I was still fuming. But then Addy curled up next to me and put her head on my shoulder. I put my arm around her. Pretty soon, our breathing slowed and I guess we both dozed off.

Lila's voice startled me awake. "Are you and Adelaide sleeping?"

"Huh?" It took me a moment to regain my senses. "What's wrong?"

Lila eased herself down on a seat in front of us and sighed. "James and Evelyn told me they're leaving at first light."

"Good riddance!" I muttered, rubbing my face.

Addy untangled herself from my embrace, got up and stretched. "What are they going to do?" she asked. "I mean, where would they even go?"

"Well, I think they're damned fools, Adelaide." Lila took a deep breath. "Or maybe *we* are for staying here. I don't know."

"Not having that trigger-happy chick and her psycho buddy around can only be a blessing," I said.

Even in the dim light inside the van, I could see Lila's shoulders droop. "I had hoped we could all work together," she said. "I failed. I thought I could organize our…our crazy group. But I failed."

Addy sat down next to her, touching her shoulder. "You didn't fail. Sometimes you just can't make people cooperate." Addy looked up at me. "Good people always keep trying. But sometimes it just doesn't work."

I really couldn't get why Lila felt the way she did, and I didn't want to think too hard about the coded message from Addy. I was beat. All I wanted to do was close my eyes and hope tomorrow would be a better day.

"Why don't we let those two keep an eye out for Pineys and coyotes and bandits," I said, stifling a yawn.

"I'm going to sleep." With that, I curled up in the back seat and shut my eyes.

I dreamt I was working on a stone wall out in a field. As I shaped and stacked the stones, I kept looking at the sky. Dark clouds were moving in fast, taking away the light. I kept working, trying to finish before the storm hit. Then a loud clap of thunder sounded and it woke me up. That's when I heard the second gunshot.

Addy sprang up and grabbed Lila's arm. They scrambled to the front of the van. I stumbled after them toward the door, still trying to separate dream from reality.

It was a strange hour. Not still night, but not yet dawn. And the fog. It seemed to catch in the tree trunks, then drift across the road in waves. There was no color in the world. Everything was gray.

Our campfire had gone out. And in the mist, I saw Jimmy and Eve running up the road toward a figure sprawled on the pavement.

Addy let out a scream, and Lila whispered, "Dear Lord, they shot the Piney!"

Addy and Lila stayed behind as I rushed to see what had happened. By the time I reached them, Jimmy was kneeling next to the body – the corpse. It was obvious he was dead. Eve, her pistol still in her hand, gagged, then stumbled to the side of the road and threw up.

I had to look. I couldn't not look. The guy was on his

back, with his legs at an odd angle. He was shot twice – once in the shoulder and once in his face. He still had his cap on. Blood pooled in his eye sockets and ran down his face, soaking the collar of his jacket and spreading onto the pavement. In the dim pre-dawn light, the blood looked black. An old baseball bat was lodged under his body.

"Oh God, no," Jimmy wailed. "We shot our driver. We shot J.J."

I heard Lila and Addy walking up. I didn't want them to see this…horror…so I pulled a red kerchief from my pocket – I always carry one with me, force of habit I guess – and covered the disfigured face. Almost instantly, the blood seeped through.

Addy came up next to me. "Is it really J.J.?"

"His face is…," I said. "He was shot in the face."

Jimmy stood up. "We didn't know. We…we thought it was the Piney with a rifle." He looked at Addy and me, maybe trying to get some kind of confirmation from us.

Something struck me at that moment. "Why do you keep saying 'we'?"

Jimmy's face was wooden, like I was speaking in a foreign tongue or something.

"You keep saying *we* shot him and *we* didn't know," I said. "I'm guessing it was Eve who shot him."

Jimmy shook his head. "I spotted him first, coming at us in the fog. I saw this shape, this guy with a rifle…I guess it was that baseball bat. I didn't know. I…I told Eve to stop him." He looked down at the wet pavement, the blood and pine needles.

Addy knelt next to the body. She hesitated a

moment, then lifted his dead hand in hers. "Into your hands, O Lord, we commend his spirit. May J.J. find eternal rest in heaven. Amen." She rose and took hold of my shoulder to steady herself.

Lila joined us as we stood around the body. "There's so much blood," she murmured.

Eve walked out of the shadows and stood next to Jimmy, looking like she was about to faint. She spoke in a hoarse whisper. "I have to turn myself in."

Chapter Twenty-One

I'm sorry, but I need to stop now. I can't go on. I need some time. I haven't told anyone about this other than my daughter. *Merda*! It's harder than I thought, reliving all this. Give me some air, please. I'll come back and continue. I promise.

Okay, let me pick up where I left off – with all of us standing around this corpse in the road, trying to figure out what to do next, trying not to get blood on our shoes.

The knowledge of what we did – what I did – back there, back then, it follows me. It's always there. Every day. I can pretend, sometimes, that it didn't happen, or it doesn't really affect me, but *mio Dio*, I know that's not true.

This is my way of trying to come to terms with everything. I guess that … well, there may be some repercussions from what I'm recording here, but I need to get this out. Okay, take a breath.

Neil MacNeill

Chapter Twenty-Two

"What do we do now?" Lila asked.

"I have to explain what I did … to the authorities," Eve whispered. "The police or someone. I didn't mean to kill him. Not J.J."

Jimmy put his arm around her. "Of course you didn't. You thought it was that Piney who shot me."

I looked over at Addy and Lila, trying to see if they were taking all this in, if they were buying it. I closed my eyes and let out a breath. "You could've … you should've shot into the air," I said. "A warning shot. You didn't have to kill him." Eve was staring into space, her eyes wide and unfocused.

Jimmy spoke up for her. "It was self-defense."

I raised my eyes to the foggy sky. Maybe I felt sorry for Eve at that moment, or maybe I didn't. I can't say for sure. But what Jimmy said set me off. "Self-defense? Really? Defense against what – a guy with a baseball bat?"

Eve broke into tears, and Jimmy hugged her closer,

looking at me with venom in his eyes. I took a few steps away from the group.

"What do we do now?" Lila repeated, as if she hadn't heard anything we'd said.

No one responded, so I turned to Lila. "We can't just leave the body here," I said. "Coyotes will get him. I saw what they did to that deer. We've got to do something."

That didn't seem to register with anyone. But then Addy said, "We should bury him."

"What?" I couldn't believe what I was hearing. "This is…this is a crime scene."

Jimmy glared at me. "You son of a bitch," he snarled.

"Okay. Okay, I didn't mean to say…" I stopped myself.

"Maybe it's manslaughter," Lila said. She seemed to come out of her shock. We all looked at her. "Well, I don't know all the legal terms," she said, "but surely you don't think Eve planned to kill J.J.?"

I guess that was a rhetorical question because no one answered.

"He deserves a proper Christian burial," Addy said.

Eve spoke again. "I have to confess … to the police."

My thoughts were racing, trying to figure out what we could possibly do, what choices we had given our situation.

Jimmy spoke up. "Maybe what we need is a temporary solution," he said. "So, I agree with Joe."

Now it was my turn to be defensive. "What the hell do you mean? You agree with me about what?" I could feel my blood rising.

Addy intervened. "Calm down, Joe." She pressed a

hand against my chest.

"Okay, let's hear what you have to say, James." Lila spread her arms out, as if to encompass not just our group, but the whole situation. She had a hard smile on her face. "Tell us about this solution of yours. Please." There was an edge in her voice, but I don't think Jimmy caught it.

"So, listen up." Jimmy pulled himself away from Eve and paced back and forth. "Joe was right – we can't just leave the body here."

"You mean J.J.'s body," Addy said. "We have to give the dead the respect they deserve."

Jimmy went on. "We need to move the body out of the road and at least cover him up so the coyotes won't get to him. A temporary solution. Okay?"

Eve was standing by herself now, whimpering. "What am I going to do?" Her arms hung limp at her sides.

"I'm getting to that, Evie." Jimmy was oblivious to her condition, her shock.

"I'd say the first thing you should do, Evelyn, is put that pistol away." Lila pointed at the weapon.

Eve looked down, her eyes wide. She still held the gun in her right hand. Her expression changed to a grimace, as if she'd picked up something foul from the road. She took a few steps away from us, and with a guttural yell, threw the gun into the woods. Either the fog muffled the sound or the dense undergrowth swallowed it up. I never heard it land.

"What did you do that for?" Jimmy rushed over and grabbed her arms. "We still need to defend ourselves.

That's our only weapon!"

Eve started to cry. "I don't want it anymore." Tears were streaming down her cheeks. "I don't want to have anything to do with it." Jimmy sighed and embraced her, and she became a lifeless doll in his arms.

A memory flashed into my mind – holding my sobbing daughter when her pet rabbit died. At that moment, Eve seemed so young, so lost.

Lila broke the silence. "I'm sorry, everyone, but I'm not feeling well. I need to eat something. For my condition." She turned and walked into the fog, back toward our van. She still had a slight limp, but I don't think that's why she was walking so slowly.

Addy grabbed my hand and led me away from Jimmy and Eve. "We have to do something with J.J.'s body," she said. "We can't leave him in the road. It's not right. It's not the right thing to do."

I nodded. "Maybe we should put him in the van."

I could see she considered this, but then shook her head. "I don't mean to be disrespectful to J.J., but that could be pretty awful for us." She paused. "The blood. The smells. No, we need to dig a grave."

I opened my mouth to protest, but she kept on talking.

"I mean a shallow grave, Joe. A temporary grave." She let that sink in. "Think about it," she said. "We don't know how long it will be … you know, until we're rescued."

"Rescued? Who the hell is going to come looking for us? The whole world may be in shambles. I don't think we're high on anyone's priorities."

We both stopped talking and looked around at the trees, our only companions in this nowhere place. Water glistened on the sharp spikes of the pine needles. Splotches of dampness darkened their bark, looking way too much like the blood stains on the pavement.

"Hope springs eternal," Addy said, her voice tired.

"Yeah, I guess. But how will we dig a grave anyhow? We don't exactly have a shovel or anything."

"Maybe we do."

I gave her a quizzical look.

"Maybe … the dog-dish hubcaps on the van," she said.

"Dog dish?"

She let out a very unfeminine snort. "You don't know that term, do you, Joe? Those sort of half-hubcap on the van, you know, the ones that just cover up the lug nuts. We used to call them dog-dish hubcaps." A spark returned to her voice. "If we can pry them off, they might work."

I could picture myself digging a small hole with a trowel, but hubcaps? Maybe if there weren't too many roots in the ground …

"It can work, Joe. When I was a little girl in Virginia, I used to sneak into the kitchen and steal the lids from under the stove. The big ones were really good for digging holes in the backyard, making a miniature excavation site for my toy trucks."

"You really were a tomboy, weren't you?"

Any pleasure I felt from our brief exchange drained away when I turned and saw the dead body still there, lying in the road. It was all too real. And we couldn't just turn our backs on this and pretend. We had to deal with it.

If the world hadn't stopped. If we hadn't gone to that seminar in Batsto. If we weren't in some godforsaken corner of South Jersey. If, if, if. What would normally happen now? Police. Questioning. And arrests. Then what would Eve and Jimmy say? Accidental shooting? Self-defense from some kind of imagined threat? None of that mattered now. There were no police here or even a park ranger. We had to deal with this as best we could. And pray that scenes of death like this weren't playing out at home.

I rubbed a hand across my face, wiping away the sweat and early-morning dew. "God hates a coward," I mumbled, and walked over to where Jimmy and Eve were deep in conversation. He was holding her shoulders at arm's length, as if scolding her or teaching her a lesson. They didn't look like lovers now – more like father and daughter.

"Okay, Jimmy, let's figure out how to do this," I said.

He let go of Eve's shoulders, and a hesitant smile appeared on his face. "You mean ... like I said? A temporary grave?"

"Yeah, with the emphasis on *temporary*."

Addy stood over the body, staring down at it. I have to admit, she had more guts than I did. I just wanted to look away. "What's the story with that baseball bat?" she said.

"What do you mean?" Jimmy seemed flustered.

"Well..." Addy took a moment to gather her thoughts. "The way he fell. When J.J. was shot, he fell backwards. So, how is the bat behind him? And what was he doing with a bat? I don't remember J.J. having one."

"What is this, CSI?" Jimmy stepped closer to Addy, as if his *minuscolo* 5-foot 4-inch frame would intimidate her. "Maybe he picked up the bat from the side of the road. Maybe he found it and figured he'd use it to defend himself."

I didn't want to look at my blood-soaked kerchief on his face, but I edged closer to the body, and for the first time noticed the dark straps over the shoulders of his black jacket. "He's got a backpack on," I said. "I guess he had the bat shoved into it." I looked up to see if anyone agreed with me. "I don't know where he got it, but that's why the bat's behind him."

Addy raised her head and looked at me. "That makes sense." She moved closer to get a better look. Addy seemed so matter-of-fact about death. It was kind of unnerving. "How in hell are you so comfortable with dead bodies?" I asked.

The tiniest smile appeared at the corners of her mouth. "My uncle was a funeral director. Back home," she said. "I spent a couple of summers helping him when I was in high school. That, and my faith."

"Your faith?" Jimmy wasn't about to let us take over the conversation.

"Of course," Addy said. "When you trust in God and truly believe He's prepared a place for you when you die, well … the Bible says it best: 'And death shall have no dominion.'"

"Yeah, I guess," I grumbled.

"You know, we should figure out what's in that

backpack," Jimmy said.

The thought of getting into the blood-soaked bag disgusted me. It seemed like robbing the dead.

"Well, *he* doesn't need it anymore," Jimmy insisted. "There could be something useful in there."

Eve had been a silent witness to all this, but I could see she was more upset now. She covered her mouth and wandered away from us. Jimmy ignored her and knelt down a good arm's length from the body. I guess he wasn't so nonchalant about dead bodies, either. I'd had it up to here trying to deal with Jimmy, and I was starting to feel bad for Eve. After all, she was just a kid. So I left Jimmy and Addy to sort things out, and followed Eve into the waves of gray mist.

I caught up with her sitting on a log by the side of the road. She was bent over, staring down at her feet, hands clasped between her knees. She looked up as I approached, and whatever I was about to say left me. Her cheeks were wet with tears and her eyes still had that hollow look in them.

"My God, Joe, this is so horrible." Her voice trembled. "Shooting at a target, even one shaped like a man, it's not the same as shooting … as killing a human being. And seeing him dead on the road. Knowing I ended his life. Knowing … knowing that I did this to J.J."

There's a lot I could have said just then – rational, logical things. I wanted to tell her that in my experience, if you carry a gun you'll eventually use it. Maybe on yourself. But looking at that young woman who seemed to be melting into the ground with grief, well, it was no time for logic. I took her hands in mine.

"You felt threatened. You reacted. That's what happened."

She looked at me with wide eyes. "Do you believe that, Joe?" Her voice caught on the words.

"It doesn't matter what I believe." That might not have been the best thing to say. I'm sure she wanted to hear something more positive, more reassuring. But I wasn't going to lie to her. And, really, what difference did it make what I believed? The only thing that mattered was what she could live with.

She hung her head again.

"Why don't you go back to the van and check on Lila," I said. "You know, with her diabetes and all." As gently as I could, I lifted her head to look into her eyes. "Please, Eve. It would be helpful ... for all of us."

Eventually, she nodded, and I eased her up off the log. They say powerful emotions like grief and regret weigh on people. With Eve, it seemed like she could hardly support her own weight. Head down, she trudged toward the van. I went in the other direction, back to the dead body.

As I approached, I heard Jimmy and Addy's voices. I couldn't make out what they were saying, but it sounded like they were arguing.

Neil MacNeill

Chapter Twenty-Three

My Nonna died when I was 15. She'd been living with us for a couple of years, and had become a kind of shadow presence, trudging around the house in her robe and slippers, and mumbling to herself, mostly in Italian. That summer morning, I was still in bed when Poppa called out to me. The tone of his voice told me something was wrong.

I ran to Nonna's bedroom and found her on the floor, with Poppa standing over her. Her nightdress was all crumpled, and a trickle of blood ran from her nose. I remember I said, "What are we going to do, Poppa?" It seemed the longest time before he responded.

"You're a strong boy – *picciotto forte*, Nonna would say." His voice broke with those words. It may have been the only time I saw my Poppa cry. He cleared his throat before continuing. "You're old enough to look at death. Help me pick her up and put her on the bed. I don't want your Momma to see her this way."

A couple years later I'd be working in the meat-packing plant in Philly. I handled plenty of freshly butchered meat and dealt with lots of blood that summer. But dead animals and dead people, well, they're not the same at all.

Jimmy and Addy both clammed up when I joined them. It was pretty obvious they were at odds. Jimmy turned to me and asked, "Aren't you hungry, Joe?"

He didn't need to seed that thought. My stomach felt like Garibaldi's tomb. "Of course I am, *boombots*! But looking at that body … I don't exactly have an appetite right now. So, what? What are you suggesting?" I looked to Addy for help, but she didn't meet my gaze. She just stared down at the body.

My thoughts were still wrapped up in my conversation with Eve. Then the obvious hit me. "This is still about the backpack, isn't it?"

Jimmy paced back and forth, his usual move when he was trying to make his case with us. Unlike Addy, he was doing all he could to *not* look at the body. "Here's my point, Joe," he said. "We don't know where J.J. got that backpack…"

"Or the baseball bat," I said.

"Yeah, the bat, too. But he either found that backpack, stole it or someone gave it to him. And either way, he held onto it for a reason."

"And that means what?"

Jimmy threw up his arms in exasperation. "That means, Joe, that besides a baseball bat, he probably has something vital in it. Maybe food."

I took a closer look at the body. The road was slick from the rain and fog. Blood pooled onto the pavement, filling the voids between the sand and tar. I tried to look past all that and consider the backpack under him. His body covered it completely, so it wasn't very big. And maybe there *was* something useful inside. But the blood. It was surely soaked with his blood.

I closed my eyes and tried to think more clearly. Did he steal the backpack or just find it alongside the road? Hey, I grew up in South Jersey, and people threw out all sorts of things when they drove through the Pines. It was the easiest way to get rid of stuff they couldn't put out to the curb for the garbage man. It wasn't unusual to see old furniture, car parts or discarded clothing on the side of the road. Or if they were a bit more discreet, just a little ways down a dirt road.

"Addy, what do you think?" I asked.

She took a moment to look up. "Whatever we do, I just want to treat J.J.'s earthly remains with respect."

"For Christ's sake, Addy," Jimmy burst out. "I'm just talking about getting into that backpack!"

"Don't use the Lord's name in vain," she spat back.

"Okay." I took a breath. "Okay. We treat his body with respect … and all that. But let's try to…get that backpack out from under him. And then we'll figure out what to do next."

"Now you're talking," Jimmy said.

"Addy? Are you okay with that?"

She nodded.

It was my turn to pace back and forth. To be honest,

the thought of touching that dead body freaked me out. Then I had another MacGyver moment.

"Jimmy. Do you still have that survival tool in your pocket?"

"The one that saved my life when the Piney shot me?"

"*Merda!* Jimmy, let that go. Do you have it or not?"

He didn't reply, but pulled it out of his pocket. I reached for it, but he turned away from me, like a spoiled little kid hoarding his toys.

"What are you going to do with it?" he asked.

"If that knife edge is sharp enough, I'm going to try to cut the straps off the backpack. And if that works, maybe we can slide it out from under him without touching the body."

He nodded. "Let me do that," he said.

"What? You don't trust me with your special tool?"

"Ha! I don't trust you with anything, Joe!"

"*Vai all'inferno!*"

"What's that mean?" His face turned red.

"I think you get the gist of it, Jimmy. Let's just see if you can cut the straps."

Addy and I gave him a wide berth as he circled around the body, bending over, then straightening up. He looked like he was trying to figure out how to pull a worm from a rosebush without getting pricked. Finally, he knelt alongside the body, opposite the shoulder wound – less blood there, I thought. With the survival tool in one hand, he reached out with his other to grab one of the thin straps. Then he stopped, his hands shaking. "I can't do it!" he sobbed and crawled away on his hands and knees.

Addy stepped forward. "You really are a wuss," she said. "Who needs your damned tool!"

I wouldn't have been more surprised if she used the F word. I mean, it wasn't exactly profanity, but coming from Addy, it might as well have been.

She got down on all fours, right up next to the body, and pulled on the shoulder strap nearest her. With her other hand, she bent his arm at the elbow so it would ease through the strap. "Let's get this over with before rigor mortis sets in," she murmured. Then she looked up at me. "Help me out, Joe."

I felt small. Like a teacher had just called on me when I hadn't done my homework. "Um … what do you want me to do?"

Addy looked down and shook her head. "Come on, Joe. Just get down here and grab hold of that bat."

I can't say I leapt to help her. Like I said, I wanted to keep my distance from that corpse. But it was Addy asking. And I sure as hell didn't want her to call me a wuss, too.

"Okay. Okay, I can do that." I moved around to his blood-covered head, crouched down and grabbed the handle of the bat. Addy moved over to the other side of the body, and as nonchalantly as taking off a coat, she slipped the strap from his shoulder and eased his other arm out.

"I'll lift him up," she said, pushing her hands under his body. "When I give you the word, use that bat to slide the backpack out." She looked me in the eye. "That way you won't get blood on you."

143

I was embarrassed to realize she saw my weakness, my fear.

I looked down at the kerchief on his face, stained a deep red, and almost threw up. Closing my eyes, I tried to control myself. On Addy's command, I leveraged the bat to one side, hoping her idea would work. The wet pavement and the blood…I guess they acted like grease. It took surprisingly little effort to slide the backpack out. Addy let out a small grunt as she lowered the body back down to the pavement.

A cop once told me that crime-scene blood smelled like licking a penny. That never made sense to me until that moment in the Pines. I tried to breathe through my mouth, but that didn't help. I felt a sharp metallic taste on my tongue, and the foulness went deep into my throat. Maybe it was more than just blood I was smelling. I put a wrist to my mouth to try to block it, but that didn't work. So I grabbed the bat again, scooted over and slid the backpack farther from the body. "*Basta*," I mumbled. A chill went down my back. "I'm done with that." I felt so numb. Like I wasn't really there. Someone else was me.

Now that Addy and I had done all the work, and the backpack was further away from the body, Jimmy walked over to it and sat down cross-legged. "Let's see what good old J.J. picked up," he said. Twitching his shoulders, he stretched out his arms as if he was getting ready to play a concerto on a Steinway. With his thumbs and forefingers acting like pincers, he reached down and unzipped the main compartment. All that drama was probably so he wouldn't get his fingers bloody.

"So," he said, "what do we have here? Hmm. Not exactly the 10 essentials, but it will do."

He looked up at us, waiting for a response. Of course I was curious, so Addy and I let Jimmy have the spotlight with this new "prize" – at least for a moment. We crouched down next to him, but before we could look inside, he zipped up the flap again, waiting for us to get settled. What a *stronzino*!

I was so fixated on the backpack, I didn't hear Lila walk up to us. "So, James," she said, *"you're* in charge of doling out the goods from J.J.'s backpack?" She held a cross-shaped lug wrench in her right hand. While she didn't hold it in a menacing way, it gave her some authority.

Eve walked out of the fog and stood by Lila's side. "I want the bat," she said. "It will remind me of what I did."

Jimmy smiled up at her. "That's fine, Evie. Whatever you want."

It was time to speak up before this became the Eve and Jimmy show. "Let's just pull everything out," I said. "Lay it on the road here and see what we have. *Then* we'll figure out who gets what."

The five of us stood around in a circle – Eve next to Jimmy, Addy next to me, and Lila by herself, slapping the lug wrench into the palm of her hand. Nobody said anything for a while as we looked down at the piddling collection of stuff. Then Lila spoke up. "All that fuss over *this*."

Laid out on the pavement was a package of granola bars, six of them, as it turned out. A folded-up plastic rain poncho in a little Ziploc pouch. A camp knife in a nice leather sheath – I was sure Jimmy would want that. A coil of garden twine. And a water bottle that had been crushed, probably from the fall. There was also an apple and a couple dollar bills held together with a paper clip, but they were both coated with a pinkish ooze of blood and water. Maybe we could clean the apple, but what good was the money to us at this point? Not even Jimmy would sink low enough to literally rob the dead.

I glanced over at Addy and realized how bedraggled she looked. I guess we all did. Then I looked down at her hands. "Addy?"

She met my gaze. "You've got blood on your hands."

A sad smile appeared on her face. "We all do, Joe. We all do."

Chapter Twenty-Four

"Well, people, let's sort this out." It was good to see Lila taking control again. She was our North Star. "Let me start the debate," she said.

I looked at her sideways, but then I got her drift.

"Okay. I'm going to take everything for myself," she said.

"Like hell you will!" snarled Jimmy. "I want that knife."

"Leave it alone, Jimmy," Eve whispered.

"She just wants us to work things out," Addy said. "Isn't that right, Lila?"

"You catch on quickly, Adelaide. That's it, alright."

"So..." I blew out a breath. "No need to play King Solomon here. There's six granola bars in that package, so we can each take one, and maybe leave another for Lila. You know, for her diabetes."

"That sounds fair," Addy said.

I waited for the others. "Jimmy and Eve, are you okay with that?"

Jimmy nodded, and Eve uttered an okay. She didn't

seem to have enough strength to speak out loud.

"That's one down," I muttered.

"We should use the rain poncho to wrap J.J.'s body," Addy said. "It might make it easier to recover him from the grave when help arrives."

I had no illusions about "help" arriving, but I liked the idea of covering up the body with the poncho. I might be able to handle the whole burial thing better that way.

"That's a fine idea, Adelaide," Lila said. "I suggest we put the twine in the bus. I'm sure we'll have some use for it. So, let's call that communal property." She paused. "Any objections so far?"

I heard a mumbled grunt from Jimmy. Addy and Eve said nothing.

"I know I'm leaving the most contentious object for last, people, but can we agree that the water bottle is useless, and for that matter, so is the cash. I suggest we put the cash in J.J.'s pocket and just … well, just bury it with him."

All I could think was "blood money." I know that's not what the phrase means, but that's what went through my head. "That's fine, Lila," I said. "A couple of dollar bills are no use to us out here. Unless we hold on to them for toilet paper."

"Joseph! Really, now."

I'm sure my face turned red when she scolded me. I just said what was on my mind, that's all.

"So that leaves the knife," Lila continued.

And here comes the argument, I thought.

"Why shouldn't I get it?" Jimmy seemed so cocksure of himself.

"You gotta be kidding me!" I said. "You already have that survival tool. And I'm not sure I agree with Eve taking the bat, but let's say she wants it for self-defense or something like that. Why the hell should *you* get the knife?"

"Joe, calm down," Addy whispered, but I wasn't about to.

"So, what, big boy? You think *you* should have it?" Jimmy squared off against me.

"I sure as hell think I'll be more responsible with it," I said. "I won't go sticking it into some phantom that I can't even see in the fog."

Jimmy's face contorted, and he charged me. I saw it coming, so I braced myself. I thought about slamming my fist into his face, but when he came at me with arms flailing – well, the *ragazzino* didn't even know how to fight. At the last moment, I sidestepped and shoved him hard. He crumpled to the pavement, cussing a blue streak the whole time.

"Joseph, stop!" Lila stepped between us, but she didn't have to. Jimmy didn't get up right away, and Eve walked over and put a hand on his shoulder.

"Let it go, Jimmy," she said. "We don't need that knife. We don't need anything here."

While all this drama was going on, I watched Addy bend down and pick up the knife. Good move, I thought. Eve glanced over, and I'm sure she saw what Addy did. She didn't say anything, though. Jimmy was crouching on the road, his breathing still ragged. Eve spoke to him, but she was looking straight at us. "Come on, let's just deal with this burial and then we can leave."

"So, you really are planning on leaving us?" Lila asked.

"Why the hell shouldn't we?" Jimmy may have been down, but he was still defiant.

Lila put one hand on her hip and used the other to point the lug wrench at them. "Well. Not to put too fine a point on this, James, but you egged her on. And Evelyn, you shot J.J."

Eve looked down at the pavement, shaking her head back and forth. She didn't offer any defense. Jimmy looked like he could spit nails.

"Before you say anything, James, I realize the shooting was a mistake. Maybe not exactly accidental, but a mistake. So, what's the plan? We bury the body and you just leave? That doesn't seem right to me."

Jimmy spoke through gritted teeth. "We need to do something. We can't just stay here and wait. Wait for what?" He looked down at the pavement and lowered his voice. "Eve and I are going to head back the way we came. We should eventually get to Batsto. At least there are houses and shelter there." He looked up and seemed to consider his next words carefully. "We'll try to find someone to help us – all of us. We're not doing this for ourselves." I caught the slightest smile on his face. Or maybe it was a sneer.

"Ha!" I couldn't believe his bullshit. "So, you're suddenly thinking of the group – all of us – instead of just yourself? Yeah, right!"

"Please!" Addy stepped closer to Jimmy and Eve, the sheathed camp knife still in one hand. "Stop all this bickering." She waved the knife in front of her as she talked, and I caught Jimmy eying it. "We have a job to do now, an obligation to deal with J.J.'s earthly remains."

"Okay, people," Lila said. "So, what's the plan? How do we deal with, you know, J.J.'s 'earthly remains'?"

Addy tucked the knife into the back of her waistband. "We start by protecting his body." She bent down, picked up the rain poncho, and shook it out. It was a lot bigger than it looked when it was all scrunched up. I was just glad the plastic was green and not transparent.

"Help me, Joe."

I nodded and swallowed hard, feeling the sweat form on my forehead. Here we go again, I thought.

Addy walked over to the corpse and got down on her hands and knees. "Get on the other side," she said.

I had to admire her ability to deal with all this. And I admit, it was only my macho pride that kept me from copping out. I bent down on the other side of the corpse, fighting the urge to upchuck what little I had in my stomach.

"Breathe through your mouth, Joe." Her voice was soft, almost intimate. "If you feel like throwing up, try smiling."

"Are you *pazza*?"

"Seriously, Joe, I learned that at the funeral home. Smiling uses muscles around your mouth that can keep you from vomiting."

I put a rigid smile on my face. It probably looked more ghoulish than happy. I just wanted this over with.

She draped the poncho over the body, backwards, like a hospital gown. "Grab the other side and find the armhole."

There was no way out of it. I straightened out the plastic as best I could.

"Now, do what I do." Addy looked at me with a tender smile. "It's okay, Joe, just follow what I'm doing, so you can do the same on your side."

Just like she'd done before, she grabbed the corpse's arm. It took some effort to line up the plastic sleeve, but eventually she pushed his arm into the poncho. "Now, you do it."

It may have been one of the hardest things I've ever done ... other than helping move Nonna's corpse, that is. I tried to be as mechanical as possible. But when I grabbed the dead arm, it slipped out of my hand. I closed my eyes and said a silent prayer to Saint Catherine of Siena – Nonna's favorite. Funny how you become religious when death is right in front of you.

One more time I reached down and grabbed his arm, bent it at the elbow, and then struggled to get it into the sleeve of the poncho. At one point I looked up at Addy. She had that same encouraging smile. If it wasn't for her, I'm sure I couldn't have gone through with it.

"That's good, Joe," she whispered. "You're doing alright." Once I was done, Addy took hold of both his arms and crossed them over his chest. She must have learned that at the funeral home, too. Or that's the way they did it in her church.

She looked over my shoulder and called to the rest of our group. "Jimmy. Eve. We need some help here."

"What about Lila?" Jimmy asked.

"She's still nursing that blow to her leg," Addy said.

"I'm perfectly capable, Adelaide."

"I'm sure you are," Addy replied, "but I don't want you kneeling down on that bruise."

"Do I have to do this?" Eve murmured.

"You, more than anyone, Evelyn." Lila didn't say it in a nasty way. Just kind of matter of fact. Like it was obvious.

Jimmy strutted over with his chest puffed out and hands on his hips. "So, what'd you expect me to do?" If that guy was Italian, I would have said he looked like Mussolini, challenging some insubordinate.

"We need to wrap the body," Addy said.

Jimmy glanced at the corpse. "It looks like you've already done that."

"We all need to do this. Every one of us. To protect J.J. from the elements." Addy paused, then softened her tone. "I don't know your religion, Jimmy, but please help me honor the dead … honor J.J."

Jimmy grunted, but eventually he knelt next to Addy. He probably wanted to be as far away from me as he could. Eve was whimpering again, but she knelt on my side. And against Addy's advice, Lila eased herself down and sat by the head of the corpse.

"Okay, this is better," Addy whispered. "I know it's not pleasant, but let's all tuck in the poncho under his body to keep out any flies or bugs." She turned to smile at each of us, encouraging us to continue. Lila pulled the hood of the poncho over his face. I didn't bother to see what the others did. Instead, I concentrated on my own task, easing my hands between the pavement and his body, tucking the plastic poncho under him. I had no idea if what we were doing was helpful, but at least we were all working together.

After she seemed satisfied with what we'd done, Addy spoke again, her tone soft and reverent. "Now let's have a moment of silence for J.J." I watched her lips move in prayer. So this was the real reason she wanted us to kneel next to the body. I should have known.

No one spoke, and as we waited out this awkward moment, I heard the wind pick up. I looked up at the trees. The fog was blowing away in wisps of gray, and the top branches were swaying. My Aunt Nettie always said that at dawn and dusk, the world holds its breath. Yeah, a pleasant fairy tale, and certainly not true in this case. The weather was changing, but at the time, we didn't know what that meant.

Lila was the first to move. She struggled to get up, so I rushed to help her. She's not a small woman, and we had a moment when I thought we'd tumble. Eventually, we both stood. She brushed off her clothes and cleared her throat, regaining her dignity. "Okay, let's get organized with this burial."

Addy took the cue. "Joe and I were talking, and I think we can pull the hubcaps from the van to dig a shallow grave. You know, use them like a little shovel. That, and the lug wrench should work."

Jimmy could never go along with something that wasn't his idea. "That sounds like it'll take forever."

I know I should have kept my mouth shut, but I had no patience. "What else do you have to do?" A moment passed when things could have escalated, but Lila spoke up.

"Many hands make light work, James." She had a

way of putting Jimmy in his place. "So, how about you and I go back to the van to get those hubcaps?" He grunted, probably the best we'd get out of him.

"Use the flat end of the lug wrench to pry them off," Addy suggested.

"I think I can figure that out, Adelaide. Why don't you, Joseph and Evelyn find a clearing in the woods. For the grave. We shouldn't have to carry J.J.'s body too far. Try to find a spot a little ways in, if you can."

Neil MacNeill

Chapter Twenty-Five

Nothing grows very big in The Pines. There are no massive oak trees like we have up north, with trunks so thick you can't put your arms around them. No towering Norwegian spruce. All the pine trees look stunted, diseased. Maybe it's because of the sand – not very rich soil for trees. But the undergrowth, that's a different story. It's thick with wild huckleberry, bramble bushes and ferns. All the stumps and dead branches are covered in spongy, gray moss. And vines snake between the tree trunks, hidden beneath it all, waiting to trip you.

We worked our way into the woods, looking for a temporary burial place. The sticker bushes caught on my pants, and I tripped on vines a few times, but caught myself before falling flat. I led the way, trying to break low-hanging branches and shoving away some of the bushes so Addy and Eve would have an easier time following me. Between the brambles and the vines, I'm sure we left some of our blood and skin along the way.

Addy spotted the clearing first, only about twenty feet in. It wasn't very wide, just a sandy gap in the trees and bushes. The soil looked dry and easy to dig. It would do.

I've never dug a grave before, not for a person, anyhow. But I've dug plenty of foundations for porches and retaining walls. With a good spade and some patience – maybe endurance is a better word – it's not that hard. Of course, we didn't have the right tools, so we had to improvise.

I paced out a 6-foot by 2-foot rectangle. Addy found a suitable dead branch and scratched an outline of the plot in the sand. Eve held back, leaning against a pine at the edge of the clearing, mumbling to herself. As confident and, well, proud as she seemed yesterday, that was all gone now.

I grew impatient, waiting for Lila and Jimmy to return with the lug wrench and hub caps, so I got down on my knees and started scooping up the loose sand with my hands.

"Let me help." Addy stood over me, but hesitated.

I looked up at her, and in that moment, with the sun breaking through the morning haze, lighting up her pale complexion, almost illuminating her face, I felt a wave of hope wash over me – hope for our situation. Hope for us.

"No, you wait for those hubcaps. It was your idea to use them."

That came out all wrong, and I saw her eyes harden.

"What I mean is, you have experience with the pots and lids and stuff ... from when you were a kid. You'll know how to use them best."

"Nice save, Joe." She brightened again, and I felt embarrassed by my clumsy comment.

"Look, I'm tired. We're all tired and just beat up by

this whole damn thing." I stood and wiped my palms on my pants before putting a hand on her shoulder. "But I think we've made a connection, the two of us." I looked into her eyes to see if she felt the same way. "I'm not very polished, Addy, but I just want to say, well, I think we're simpatico."

She shook her head, but her smile broadened. "You and your Italian words! Okay, we can be simpatico."

"Joseph! Adelaide! Evelyn! Where are you?" Lila's call broke our brief *intermezzo*. I wasn't surprised she couldn't find us. A dozen paces into the woods might as well have been a mile. It's easy to lose sight of things in the Pines.

"Here, Lila!" I shouted. "I'll come to you." As I looked for a clearer path out, I saw Addy walk over to Eve. I hoped she could comfort her...without getting all religious.

Digging the grave was more difficult than I imagined it would be. Even in the chilly morning air, I was sweating. I had plenty of callouses on my hands, but Addy and Lila, I'm sure they suffered with cuts and blisters that morning. The hubcaps were helpful at first, but roots just under the surface made it harder to scoop the sand. I used the pointed end of the lug wrench as a pick, striking the ground hard to break through the vines and loosen the soil around the edges of our 6-foot plot. Water's never far beneath the surface in the Pines, and as we dug further, it didn't take long for the sandy soil to become wet and heavy.

I glanced over at Eve from time to time, trying to see any change, wondering if Addy's talk with her had done any good. But she still appeared dazed and so apart from us. Jimmy was standing nearby, but they didn't seem as close as before.

I took a breather, and Addy and Lila stepped in. Jimmy and Eve never once volunteered to help, and I felt my resentment growing.

When I stood back to survey our work, I thought we'd taken a bite out of the job. The burial plot was about a foot-and-a-half deep. This was supposed to be a temporary grave, so that seemed deep enough to me. Addy and Lila stood to join me, and Lila shook her head.

"James and Evelyn, how about you take over for us and work with these hubcaps?" she said. Jimmy crossed his arms over his chest but didn't make a move to help. Then Eve stepped forward.

We all got out of her way, waiting to see how she'd handle this. At some point, she must have picked up the baseball bat. She'd probably had it behind her the whole time we were digging. I never noticed.

She stepped into the shallow grave, dropped onto her knees, and started slamming the bat into the sand, raising it over her head with two hands like she was wielding a battle axe, chopping down hard. Each time she struck the earth, she let out a rasping cry, like *she* was being hit by the bat. Her hair came undone, and loose sand sprayed into her face with each blow. She didn't seem to notice. I know I should have done something, but we were all frozen in place.

Lila cried out in a harsh whisper. "James!"

Jimmy stepped closer to the grave, but even he was hesitant. He spoke softly at first. "Evie, honey, please stop." She didn't seem to notice he was there. Again, she raised the bat over her head and slammed it down into the hard sand.

He tried once more, raising his voice above Eve's grunts and the pounding thunks of the bat hitting the ground. "Evie, calm down."

Nothing.

"Evie, you're scaring me." Jimmy threw his arms up and yelled, "Goddamn it, Eve, stop!"

As she raised the bat again, Jimmy stepped forward and grabbed it. They struggled. Eve wailed in protest. She must have been pumped with adrenaline, because she broke Jimmy's grip and banged the bat once more into the earth. The old wooden bat could only take so much abuse. It splintered, bits of wood flying into the air. Eve released the stub and collapsed into the grave, her face buried in her hands. Jimmy knelt down and reached out to her limp body. He stroked her shoulders and back, petting her like she was some sad little puppy who needed his comfort.

I felt a low, dull throb across my eyebrows. What my Nonna used to call an *emicrania*. It was all going to hell, and there was nothing I could do to stop it.

Neil MacNeill

Chapter Twenty-Six

I have a strong physical memory of that moment, and all the thoughts and feelings fighting each other in my head.

What were we doing there? What were we trying to bury…besides a body, that is. And more than anything, why was I going along with all this? The world had stopped. People had died, some horribly, like in that plane crash. More in the cities, but we didn't know that yet. And meanwhile, an innocent man walking down a country road in the early morning fog had been gunned down by another innocent, a young woman so frightened by the world that she lashed out at any harm she imagined was coming her way.

And in this murder, this too-convenient burial, I was an accomplice. The fool who went along with everything, even when I knew better. Was I doing this for Addy, for her and her religion? Or somehow to help Eve, who was so torn apart by guilt she was losing her mind?

Even after all these years, I still struggle with the decisions we made back then in the Pines. So cut off from everyone and everything.

And if Jimmy was telling you all this, if he was giving you this oral history instead of me, would it be any different? Damn right it would!

Okay, let me continue.

Eve was totally spent, and Jimmy was treating her like a pet instead of a broken woman – rubbing her shoulders and saying soothing words to her. Addy … I'm not sure what she was thinking, so I turned to Lila for some sense of reason, for some sanity in all this.

Before I could say anything, the wind picked up, and I heard a loud crack above us. A limb had snapped, high in a pine tree. It got hung up in the branches on the way down, and sent a spray of brown needles raining down on us. Just as suddenly, the wind died, and then I caught the unmistakable sound of an engine in the distance. "Addy, Lila, do you hear that?"

Addy turned toward the noise and came running to me. "Joe, that's a car. That's a car on a road somewhere…somewhere through the trees." She smiled as she grabbed my shoulders. "Someone is out there. Someone can save us."

The booming exhaust grew louder, peaked, and then faded as the car sped away.

Jimmy stood and cocked an ear to the receding sound. "Addy's right. That was no tractor. It was a car, a loud, fast car."

Addy looked like a kid who'd solved a puzzle. She turned to Jimmy. "It sounded like a small-block Chevy." She waited for his response, but he just shrugged. "A worked Chevy V8. That's what it was."

I stared at Addy. "How the hell do you know this stuff?" She gave me a sly smile. "Yeah, I know, something about your daddy's farm in Virginia ..."

We all stood still, straining to catch any last echo of the car's exhaust, but the sounds of the Pines returned – wind, birdsong and the constant creaking of tree branches rubbing against each other.

"This changes everything," Addy said.

"Damn straight it does." Jimmy started pacing back and forth in our little clearing, avoiding Eve and the grave, putting on his school teacher airs. "That guy was moving fast, so there must be another road...somewhere over there." He pointed into the woods. "A real road, not some deserted two-lane blacktop like the one we're stuck on."

Addy put a hand on my chest and smiled up at me. "We're not alone, Joe. The world might have stopped, but...maybe it restarted."

"It never stopped for the Piney," I said. "And maybe that was another Piney, just in a faster vehicle."

"Don't be such a downer!" Jimmy came back at me.

"Joseph is right about one thing." Lila joined the conversation. "That may have been a car, and I guess it was driving on some bigger road, but we have no idea what the driver was up to – good or evil."

"Now you're bringing us down, too," Jimmy said.

Lila had a haunted look in her eyes. "I've been alone

in the city…at night. You hear a loud car nearby, and it could mean a lot of things. None of them good."

Jimmy waved his hands dismissively.

"What are you trying to say, Lila?" I asked.

She looked straight into my eyes, as if we were the only two people there. "Do cop cars have loud exhausts like that? And if that was an ambulance or some kind of rescue vehicle, wouldn't we have heard a siren? We'd better be damned careful who we flag down for help, that's all."

Addy started to say something, then stopped herself.

"I think we should be glad that that car or truck was not on our road," Lila continued. "Whatever's happened out there, out in the world, maybe we're better off here – cut off from it."

I could see Jimmy biting his bottom lip, like he was itching to add to what Lila was saying, maybe with some kind of doomsday story. In the end, no one said any more. The sun broke through the morning haze, but none of us looked up at the new day. Even Addy now seemed defeated. I doubt she'd lost her conviction that some kind of divine intervention would save us, save mankind, but the gleam had gone out of her eyes.

Of course, Jimmy couldn't keep his mouth shut for long. "Yeah, whatever," he said. "But I'll tell you one thing. Just like Addy said, this changes everything. And it justifies everything Evie and I are planning. We'll walk back to Batsto Village. That's what we'll do. Stay away from any big towns. Maybe they'll be other people there who can help us."

"You mean you're not just walking from us…leaving

us here?" Addy challenged him, a surprising edge to her voice.

"Jesus Christ, Addy, we're going to get help."

"Stop being so profane, Jimmy." Addy walked away, turning her back on all of us. She lowered her voice before continuing. "And stop lying."

I'm sure Jimmy heard that last bit, but he ignored it.

My head was spinning. At first, I thought we should try to start the van again. Then I remembered all the blown fuses. No way could we get the engine running. And we sure as hell couldn't push start it like my old Chevy pickup. But someone else had figured out a way around this EMP thing. Someone had gotten a car running, and they were hell-bent on getting somewhere fast. But were they heading *to* some place ... or trying to get away from something?

"Maybe...well, maybe this does change everything," I said. "Maybe Jimmy is right, and we should all head back to Batsto, back the way we came."

"Now you're talking!" Jimmy's face lit up.

"Even if a bigger road is over there, through the woods somewhere, how are we going to get to it?" I said. "We had a hard enough time getting to this clearing." I shook my head. "No, we should probably head back to some kind of familiar shelter. To Batsto Village."

"But the grave." Addy gave me a penetrating look. "J.J.'s body. We can't leave it on the side of the road. He needs a proper burial – a Christian burial. The Bible says, 'The dust returns to the earth as it was, and the spirit returns to God who gave it.'"

I couldn't meet her gaze, but I had to get this out.

"Look, Addy. If Lila's reckoning is right, well, that means there are some bad people – people up to no good who have figured out how to bypass the effects of this EMP. And we don't want to be found by them."

"What will we do in Batsto, Joseph?" Lila stepped between Addy and me. "Nobody actually lives there. It's a historic park."

Jimmy moved closer to us. He knew how to use his body to impose himself in a conversation, even as small as he was. "There are buildings and shelter there," he said. "Maybe even running water ... at least a clean stream by the old mansion. It's better than waiting here in the middle of nowhere."

"So we just leave here with no sense of humanity?" Addy spun around to face Jimmy. I could see tears in her eyes. "With no respect for tradition, for faith?"

I should've considered before I spoke my next words, but I didn't. They just came out. "We don't know what his faith was. And does it really make a difference if we leave the body by the side of the road or we drag him into the woods to bury him?"

"Joe. Joe, what are you saying?" I think that was the moment I lost any connection with Addy. She looked betrayed. "If it were you...your mortal remains...what would you have us do?"

Christ, that really hit home. Who would be worried about me, wondering where I was in all this mess? Caring if my remains were rotting in the soil of the Pine Barrens? Certainly not my ex-wife. She had nothing to do with me anymore. My daughter? She might be worried, but she was in Ohio. And I never told her about this day trip to

Batsto. It's pretty depressing to realize no one cares what happens to you, but that's exactly what I thought right then. And it weighed on me like a ton of bricks.

"Oh, for God's sake," Lila raised her voice above our squabble. "Let's get this burial over with."

"For God's sake, indeed," Addy whispered.

There had to be better ways to carry a body. And I thought Addy, with her stint at a funeral home, would know how. But I guess funeral homes have rolling carts or something. Maybe a cop or a coroner would have a better idea. But us? We each grabbed a corner – Addy and I by his shoulders. Jimmy and Eve – she'd come out of her stupor enough to help us – grabbed his legs. Lila borrowed the knife from Addy and tried to cut away some of the small branches to make our passage into the woods easier. She wasn't very good at it, though. Not exactly a task that office managers would know how to tackle.

None of this went easy. You've heard the term, "dead weight"? I got a better understanding of it that day. And even though I was glad we had the poncho wrapped over him, it kept catching on the undergrowth, ripping to show us more blood and gore. The plastic was slick with dew, and I had to switch hands from time to time and readjust my grip. I'm not sure how Addy managed.

I got through it by narrowing my focus, forcing some kind of tunnel vision. As we trudged into the woods, I avoided looking at his head, lolling back and forth with each step. I kept telling myself he was just a big piece of meat we were carrying. Not a human. Not J.J.

When we made it to the clearing, Lila directed us. "Go slow now. That's good. Adelaide, you and Joseph set his body down first." She stepped over to cradle his head as we lowered the body next to the shallow grave. Jimmy and Eve had an easier time with his legs. And then we all stood looking at the corpse, catching our breath.

"Let's take a moment to get our strength back," Lila said, but she didn't give us much time before she had us slide the body into the grave. "Adelaide, maybe you could say a few words."

At first, Addy didn't reply. She wore a tight smile as she closed her eyes and raised her face to the sky. For a moment, I thought that would be the end of it, but then she spoke. "Please join hands."

I didn't want to do that. Not with Jimmy standing next to me. I'm sure he didn't want to either. We kind of glanced at each other, and when he reached out his hand, I took it.

"Please close your eyes as we pray," Addy continued. "To every thing there is a season, and a time to every purpose under heaven. A time to be born, and a time to die. A time to kill, and a time to heal." She paused. I thought she might be trying to remember the rest of the verse. What she said next really hit home. "God shall judge the righteous and the wicked, for there is a time for every purpose and for every work. All are of the dust, and all turn to dust again. Amen."

She knelt and grabbed some of the sandy soil,

throwing it into the grave. After an awkward pause, the rest of us did the same.

Neil MacNeill

Chapter Twenty-Seven

A tree above the clearing was bleeding on us. I craned my neck and saw a fresh wound near the top, and a big branch caught up in one of the lower limbs. Sap clung to the windblown pine needles, forming pointy tridents, horns and stars. None of this helped the job ahead of us.

As we covered up the corpse, the soil felt even wetter than before. It made me wonder how high the water level was in the Pines, and what that would mean to the decomposing body we were burying.

Jimmy and I knelt on either side of the grave, using the hubcaps to scoop up the sand. I didn't look at him, and I'm sure he avoided eye contact with me. We worked in silence, except for Addy's encouragements as she walked around the grave. My hands became sticky with sap.

I glanced up and saw Lila deep in conversation with Eve. At one point, Lila lifted a hand to Eve's cheek, brushing away a tear. It was good to see her trying to soothe Eve's misery.

The day grew hazy again. The sun cast no shadows in our little clearing. Even the usual sounds of the forest were muted. Our whole world seemed gray and lifeless. Or maybe it was just my mood.

We finished filling the hole, and I rubbed some sand between my hands to try to get rid of the stickiness. I hate the scent of pine.

Before we could move on, Addy stood at the head of the grave, closed her eyes and put her palms together in prayer. I was relieved she didn't ask us to join hands again. I was done with all that kumbaya crap. It was time to get on with the day, no matter what fate had in store for us.

Addy opened her eyes and smiled, and Lila came over to join us. "Well, that's done, at least," Lila said. "Let's get back to the van and sort things out." She glanced at Eve, still standing apart from us, and waved her over. "Come on, Evelyn. Let's get out of the woods."

Lila led the way as we fought through the undergrowth and low-hanging branches, going single-file, back toward the road. I was a couple of paces behind her, and I could see she was still walking cockeyed, favoring her "good" leg. I called out to say I'd take the lead. As she turned, her legs twisted, and she tumbled into the bushes. Addy and I rushed over and knelt beside her.

"Goddamn it, Joseph. I must have got caught up in a vine."

"It was my fault," I said. "I shouldn't have made you turn around."

"I won't hear of that, Joseph. It's all on me." She

tried to get up, but grimaced with pain.

"You just wait a moment," Addy said, laying a hand on her shoulder. "Don't move until we know where you're hurt."

"Oh, I know where I'm hurting, Adelaide," she said. "And it's right in the same place I was hurting before."

Jimmy came over and stood above us, an odd look on his face. He turned and called to Eve. "Honey, how about you go on ahead to the van and get my survival pouch. I left it under the jump seat."

Eve frowned. She looked hesitant.

"Come on, Evie," Jimmy said. "Please do this for me. Oh, and a water bottle, too."

She mumbled an okay and walked past us, dodging branches to get to the road.

Addy stood and faced Jimmy. "That's very thoughtful of you," she said. "Getting the OxyContin for Lila."

He smiled, but didn't look at Addy. He seemed to chew on his words. "Yeah, I guess. But I want to do a kind of trade."

I didn't like where this was going. "What are you talking about, Jimmy?"

Again, he wouldn't meet our eyes. He hitched up his shoulders, like James Cagney in some old gangster movie. "You know. One hand washes the other."

I stood up, my hands balling into fists. "Out with it, you little *pompinara*."

He looked straight at me. "I want the knife," he said.

Addy and I were both speechless. Lila broke the silence. "Do I understand you correctly, James?" Her voice was trembling, either from pain or emotion. "Are you really suggesting that you … won't give me any painkillers unless we give you J.J.'s knife?"

His face turned red. "It's not like that," he said.

My body tensed. I counted to 10, waiting to see where this would go, ready to jump the guy and twist his arm until he begged for mercy.

"I'm not …" he stopped and looked up at the sky. "It's just that, well, Lila won't be going anywhere now, will she? And I know how you guys stick together. So, you'll be staying here when Eve and I leave. And I just thought … well, I need the knife more than you do."

I shook my head. He was pathetic. A little fool who thought the world revolved around him. He wasn't even worth my anger. I should've pitied him. And I would've if I wasn't so damned pissed off. But then Lila and Addy surprised me. It was as if they'd planned it all in advance. Lila reached behind her, pulled the knife from her waistband, and handed it to Addy. She took the knife, straightened and extended her arm to Jimmy.

"Here, Jimmy," she said. "If it means that much to you."

His face lit up like it was Christmas morning.

"No, Addy!" I shouted. "This isn't right."

She gave me a half-hearted smile. "It's okay," she said. "We both get what we want. He gets the knife, and we get to help Lila feel better."

I started to reply, but then I heard Momma's voice in my head. "One nail drives out the other, Joey." *Merda*! I guess the women had a point. I had almost forgotten about the knife, and Lila could sure use those painkillers.

So, give Jimmy what he wants. But it still didn't sit right with me.

I heard footsteps in the undergrowth as Eve emerged between the trees, water bottle and Jimmy's survival pouch in hand. She stood silent a moment, taking in what was happening, then chucked the pouch to Jimmy. He caught it, but I could see her action surprised him. She knelt next to Lila and helped her sit up.

Lila took a couple of sips of water, caught her breath and whispered a thank you. Jimmy didn't move.

"Come on, Jimmy," I said. "*Your* side of the trade, remember?"

He turned his back as he unzipped the pouch, no doubt counting out his remaining pills and checking whatever else he had in there.

"More than *one* pill, Jimmy," I said.

He glanced over his shoulder to scowl at me, but I'm sure he knew I wouldn't let up. He zipped up his little pouch and walked over to Eve, handing her two pills.

Eve shook her head. "*You* give it to Lila."

Maybe Eve was coming out of her shock, or maybe she was starting to see Jimmy for what he really was. Either way, Jimmy was cornered now. He shuffled closer to Lila and extended his hand, two tiny white pills in his palm. To her credit, Lila took a moment before she grabbed the pills. She looked him straight in the eye and dry-swallowed one pill, then motioned to Eve for more water. Still staring at Jimmy, she tucked the other pill in a front pocket.

I decided to pile on. "So, Jimmy. This is what you were planning all along, wasn't it?"

"What do you mean?" he mumbled.

"You and Eve heading off without us. Doing your own thing. Abandoning us."

"It's not that way." His voice rose, but he still wouldn't meet my eyes.

Addy stepped in. "Which way are you going to go?" He glanced up at her. "Do you have a plan? I mean, what if you run into bad people?"

That shit-eating grin returned to his face. "That's why I wanted the knife."

"Like a knife's going to help you if a Piney has a shotgun!" I really didn't think a Piney was going to shoot at him. Heck, a Piney never *did* shoot at him. But I wasn't going to let him have the last word. The knife was more than a weapon to him. It was some kind of totem that gave him power. Never mind all that. He just didn't get it. He didn't realize how we were all looking at him.

Jimmy ignored me. "And we're going south," he told Addy. "At least I assume it's south, unless J.J. really turned us around. Back the way we came. Back toward Batsto."

Good riddance, I thought. But I wouldn't let him go before putting him to work. "Before you desert us, how about you help out?"

"What?"

"We need to get Lila back to the van. Give me a hand."

For an infuriating moment, he didn't budge. Like he could refuse! Before I could threaten him, he gave me a reluctant nod. I turned to Lila. "Do you think you can walk if we help? Jimmy and I will be on either side, supporting you. Is that okay?"

Her eyes watered. "I'm sorry to be such a burden, Joseph," she said in a small voice.

"Nonsense, Lila. You'd do the same for me, for any of us. I know you would." I turned my attention to Jimmy. "Come on, let's help her up."

It was a struggle. As I mentioned, she was no small woman, and she couldn't put much pressure on one leg, but we managed. Addy and Eve went ahead of us, parting the branches and leading us out of the woods. To his credit, Jimmy held up his end, and we hobbled along.

We'd only gone a few paces when I stepped on something hard, and for a moment I lost my grip on Lila. "What's wrong?" Jimmy asked.

"Wait a minute!" I got a better hold of Lila under her arm and glanced down to see what I'd stepped on. It was covered in pine needles and moss, but it was un-mistakable – Eve's pistol. "It's just a rock," I said.

In that instant, I'd made a choice. I knew full well there'd be consequences, that somewhere down the road, I might second-guess my choice. But I think I made the right one.

Neil MacNeill

Chapter Twenty-Eight

We broke through the trees onto the pavement, and I took a moment to catch my breath. The van seemed farther away than it should have been. Distances are deceiving in the Pines.

I had a secret now, something I promised I'd keep to myself. Maybe I'd made a moral judgment, or maybe I was concerned for everyone's safety. You decide. My gut said that Eve's gun would only get us into more trouble.

Addy picked up the box of granola bars from the pile of things on the road. She bent to get the backpack, hesitated, then kicked it to the shoulder. The rest of the meager belongings didn't seem like they'd be of any use to us. The blood-soaked apple was nowhere to be seen – probably carried away by a critter who either didn't care or was attracted by the smell.

Even though everyone seemed caught up in their own world, I couldn't shrug off the feeling that they knew I was keeping something from them. The way they glanced at me. The things they weren't saying. Secrets have a way of eating at you.

I nodded to Jimmy, and we continued our slow progress, mindful of Lila's pain when she put too much pressure on her bad leg. We eventually got to the van and settled her into the jump seat by the front bumper. Her eyes were half-closed. The rest of us looked at each other, as if waiting for someone to make the next move.

I saw Jimmy eyeing the water bottles. Five bottles were left, not counting the one Eve had gotten for Lila. Eve was still carrying that one. I turned to her, cutting Jimmy off before he could say something stupid.

"I'll take Lila's water bottle from you," I said. "You and Jimmy can each have a new one. That'll leave one each for Addy and me, and one extra for Lila."

She handed me Lila's half-empty bottle. "I guess that's fair."

Jimmy looked like he was about to choke on his words. Was he really going to demand more water? No matter, it was settled now. He snatched up two of the water bottles and gave me the stink eye.

Addy tore into the granola box and handed two of them to Eve. "So, you're on your way," she said. It was no longer a question.

Eve looked down at the ground. "I guess so. That's what Jimmy wants."

"You do what *you* want, girl." It surprised me to hear Lila speak. She wasn't as out of it as I'd thought.

Jimmy grabbed Eve's arm. "Don't listen to them, honey. Let's get going." For just a moment, I thought she might resist, but she let Jimmy lead her away.

They didn't go far before Addy shouted at them to stop. She ran over to Eve and whispered in her ear,

Jimmy frowning the whole time. Eve nodded, and they walked away, back down the road, following their own destiny.

When Addy came back, I asked her, "What did you say to Eve?"

"I told her God would forgive her."

Couldn't she think of something more constructive? But there was no point arguing with Addy, especially about her religion. We had to stick together now that it was just the three of us, and one of us was drugged up and in pain.

The morning wore on, changeless, as if time had stood still. The wind was high in the trees, and the low clouds never let the sun peek through. I felt fidgety. I wanted to do *something*, anything other than sitting around, waiting for someone to find us.

We'd been stuck in the Pines for less than a day, but it felt like much longer. And other than the Piney and that guy walking in the woods last night, the only sign of human life had been the roar of a fast car somewhere on the other side of the woods.

There was nothing else to do but stew in my own juices. And I realized I was hungry, damned hungry. What I wouldn't have given for a big bowl of pasta! Addy and I had agreed to keep the granola bars for later, but I had no idea when "later" would arrive.

"Hey, Addy." I think I startled her out of a dream.

She was sitting on the ground next to Lila, propped up against the front bumper.

"Sorry. I must have dozed off."

I gave her a moment to wake up. "You know those granola bars? Maybe we should have them now. Or maybe half. I'm starving."

She rubbed her eyes and eased herself up, arching her back to stretch. "I guess so," she said between yawns. "Maybe let's split one and share. Okay?"

I would've agreed to any portion. "Sure. You break and I'll pick."

She smiled and pulled out one of the bars, carefully opening the wrapping so she wouldn't lose any crumbs. She broke the bar evenly enough, and I took a piece.

As hungry as I was, I guess I took too big a bite. The damn thing stuck in my throat. It felt like swallowing cement mix. "Water!"

For some reason, this struck Addy as funny. She was practically in tears when she handed me a bottle. I gulped, again overdoing it, bringing on another choking fit.

"Excuse me, Joseph, but didn't your mama teach you how to chew?" All the noise we'd made woke up Lila, and drugged or not, she was sharp enough to make a joke at my expense.

"Hey, it's not funny," I said when I could talk.

"No, it's not, Joe, but sometimes you are." Addy smiled, and it brightened my mood.

Lila's expression changed in an instant. The little jibe she'd made had perked her up, but now her shoulders sagged and she stared off into space. "Do you think we'll see them again?" She whispered, like she was thinking out loud.

"Eve and Jimmy? No, I don't," I said. "Even if they find help...if they send someone to get us – and those are huge ifs – they're doing their own thing now. I don't know about Eve, but I'd wager that Jimmy never wants to set eyes on us again."

Addy's smile faded, and I could see the disappointment in her eyes. "Do you really have such a negative view of human nature?" No matter how bad things got, Addy looked at the world through rose-colored glasses. Maybe that's what made her attractive. Her hair had come undone, and her clothes ragged, torn and dirt-stained. But that didn't matter. I wanted to give her a big hug and tell her everything was going to be alright. But I knew it wasn't going to be.

I'm not a pessimist, but I've seen too much of humanity, and a lot of it isn't very pretty. I didn't want to burst Addy's bubble, but I think I had a bead on Jimmy's attitude. "It's not so much human nature as Jimmy's nature. He's in it for himself, and no one else matters. Certainly not us. And not even Eve."

Addy didn't contradict me. Lila was too lost in thought to say anything more. The conversation died, and I became aware of the wind in the trees. It was breezy where we stood in front of the van, but the wind was much stronger in the treetops. Branches creaked against each other. It made me nervous. The pine trees weren't very tall, but if one of the bigger limbs came down, it could do a person damage. Then I heard another sound – a distant rumble, deep and throaty. It was getting louder. "Listen! That's a truck!"

The sound grew and grew. And, just as quickly, receded, fading into the distance. Heading toward where I wanted to go. North. Toward home.

Chapter Twenty-Nine

"*Merda! Merda! Merda!* Another goddamn vehicle goes roaring by ... on that road over there, on the other side of the pines, past all the dead limbs and sticker bushes and swamps. It sounded so close, but it might as well be 100 miles away for all the good it does us." I was so frustrated, I stomped my feet on the ground. "And we're stuck here, waiting for some good-hearted soul to drive down this goddamn piece of shit South Jersey road and rescue us."

"Joe, please. Don't use the Lord's name ..."

"Yeah, I know, in vain. But that sums up everything we've done here. It's all in vain. It doesn't make a goddamn ... make a damned bit of difference. It means nothing and gets us nowhere."

"Surely, Joseph ... surely it's a good sign." Now it was Lila's turn to go all optimistic on me. "Cars and trucks are back on the road. They've managed to get past this...this EMP thing. And they're driving again. People are driving again."

I spit on the ground. Bits of granola came out and

stuck to the dead pine needles at the edge of the road. It was hard to say out loud what I was thinking, but I was losing faith in our prospects of getting out of there. It all comes down to two choices in a situation like ours – move or stay put. "Look, I hate to say this, but maybe Jimmy had the right idea."

Addy's eyes widened. "I can't believe what I'm hearing. What about, you know, Lila and her leg? How are we going to get anywhere?"

"We can work something out, Addy. Maybe find a branch strong enough to support her weight."

"People! I'm right here!" Lila leveraged herself up from the jump seat. "Don't go talking about me as if I'm invisible." She seemed genuinely insulted. I had a flash of insight into what it must have been like to be a Black woman working in an office of white men. But I didn't dwell on it. "I can manage," she said. "That is, if we really want to leave."

"Lila's right, Joe. I'm sure we can fashion a cane or walking stick out of a dead branch. But that's not the issue. I mean ... do we really want to leave this place? It's shelter from the elements. And from whatever else is out there in the woods."

They had a point, but whatever patience I had was gone. All I could picture was that truck we'd heard. I could see it driving up Route 206, heading toward my home in North Jersey. I could picture myself in that truck. And then I'd be away from this crazy place.

"Look ..." I started walking around in circles, trying to get my thoughts together. "Look at this road we're on. Take a good look. Do you think it's well-traveled? Even if this EMP disaster hadn't happened, do you think we'd see more than one or two cars drive by all day? We're in the middle of nowhere, for God's sake!"

"Joe, please ..."

"Yeah, okay. I'm sorry about cussing, but I can't take this waiting anymore."

I let all this sink in. No point arguing with the two women. They would either come around to my way of thinking or not. In the meantime, just in case the ladies did agree to leave, I started looking around for a big branch – oak, not pine – that would make a good cane.

Most of the trees in the Barrens are Pitch Pine. I learned that years later. They can survive forest fires because of their thick bark. Some sprout new branches after a fire, even when they're blackened and look dead. The few oak trees are much stronger, but they don't survive wildfires. I know there's some strange metaphor in all that, but I'll be damned if I know what it is. And I'm getting ahead of myself.

I wandered up the road, past the discarded backpack and smears of blood and gore on the road – trying not to look at any of it – searching for an oak branch. I didn't want to venture into the woods again, so it took me a while until I found a dead limb, about 4 feet long. It may not have been oak, but it wasn't pine. When I smacked it on the pavement, it didn't crack. It would do.

I started heading back to the van, thinking about how

I could convince the ladies that we should leave.

The smell crept up on me. It didn't seem that strong at first, kind of like waking up at a campsite and noticing the doused fire from the night before – wet ashes, and maybe a few dying embers. I looked up at the hazy sky, and for the first time wondered if what I was seeing was not mist or clouds ... but smoke.

If I had my bearings right, the wind was now blowing from the north. That could only mean the fire, the forest fire, was coming our way.

Merda! Yeah, I said that a lot. You want it in English? Okay, shit! We were in deep shit now.

Chapter Thirty

I came running back to the van, out of breath, and yelled, "Fire!" At first, Addy and Lila didn't believe me. They just stared at me like I was *pazzo*.

"Look up! That's not mist – it's smoke!"

"Are you sure, Joseph? I don't smell smoke."

"Maybe the wind was blowing the other way, or we've gotten used to the smell." I dragged my palm across the hood of the van. Its silver-gray paint was dull from sitting out in the elements, but when I looked at my hand, it wasn't dirty, it was black. I put it to my nose, and the smell was unmistakable. "That's not pine dust or some crap from the woods. That's soot!"

Addy and Lila stared at the streak I'd left on the hood, as if hoping to find some way to contradict me. I waited, letting it sink in, until my emotions got the better of me.

"Look. Look up in the trees. The wind's shifted. It's coming from the north now – that way." I pointed up the road, to what I assumed was north. "The fire is that way. Maybe from the plane crash. Maybe from something else. I don't know. But we've got to move. We've got to head south. To get away."

"You mean follow Eve and Jimmy?" Addy looked at me wide-eyed.

"As a matter of fact, yes."

I took in our situation. It was like I was seeing it for the first time. A broken-down van with a jury-rigged jump seat propped against the front bumper. A few water bottles and granola bars. A jumble of charred branches in the middle of the road from our campfire. In less than 24 hours, this had become our home base, our only sense of security. It was pathetic.

"Okay, let's get organized, then." Lila may have had a bum leg, but she was still set on "managing" our way out of there. "Adelaide, you go back inside the van and find anything you think we might need. Rip it out so we can take it with us." She turned to me. "Joseph, take a closer look at the toolkit. See if there's something more useful than a jack in there."

"Do you still have the lug wrench?"

"It's right here under my seat."

I nodded. That would be a useful tool and a decent weapon if need be. Yeah, I know, not as good as a gun or knife, but it could do some damage in a fight.

"I'll see if I can think of anything else, and practice using that big branch you found for me to walk with."

"I don't think we have much time," I said.

"I know that. So get to work!"

The toolkit wasn't in the back by the spare tire. As Lila suspected, the only thing back there was a hydraulic jack – no use to us as far as I could figure. I walked around to the front passenger door and saw that we'd already scavenged the lug wrench from the toolkit under the seat. The rest of its contents were pretty meager. Maybe the fleet company figured roadside assistance would take care of any problem. I dumped everything onto the floor, hoping to find some road flares. No such luck.

As I knelt on the ground by that front passenger seat, sorting this stuff out, Addy walked up the aisle between the front seats and grabbed the rearview mirror, trying to yank it free. It was a high-roof van, so she had plenty of room to get a good grip on it, but the mirror wouldn't budge. She hiked up her pant legs, planted one foot on the dashboard for better leverage, and put some muscle in it. Her pants were ripped in places, and her knees were surely bruised if not bloody, but none of that got in the way – she was dead set on pulling that mirror off. With an angry grunt, she tugged at it again. Nothing.

There I was, down on my knees by the passenger door, taking it all in. From my vantage point, well, I let my eyes take in her shape, how fit and trim she was – *snella* – but with curves in all the right places.

Was I more attracted to her because of the disaster we were living through? Probably. But my desire for her was real. "You have a delightful figure," I said, smiling up at her.

Another woman might have been pissed off, maybe even thrown something at me. Enough had passed between the two of us that Addy took it in stride. She gave me a frustrated look, but there was a smile behind it. "That's nice of you, Joe, but how about you quit admiring my figure and help me take off this mirror."

"I'm at your service."

"Is there a screwdriver in that toolkit?"

"Mm-hm." I grabbed the van's reversible screw driver and stepped into the cab.

"The mirror's embedded in this plastic housing. I don't know how to get it out."

"Let me try."

Addy still had her hands on the mirror, so I stood behind her, using the screwdriver to pry apart the plastic trim while she pulled. I struggled for a moment, then dropped the screwdriver and put my arms around her. She leaned into me and wrapped her arms around mine. I closed my eyes, thinking of anything but the mirror.

"Do you think we'll get out of here okay?" she whispered.

"If the wind doesn't pick up. If it gets windy, well...we can't stay here. Maybe we can find our way to the state highway."

Our embrace felt so good, so reassuring, even though we had nothing to be reassured about. Just two people holding on to each other. Two people who cared for each other and were looking out for each other. That gave me hope. I didn't want to let her go.

"When you two are done, we need to get a move on." Lila stared at us through the windshield, one hand on her hip, the other holding her makeshift cane.

Her words broke the spell. Addy stepped down from the van, and I scrambled to find the screw-driver again. We avoided each other's eyes. "I'll take down that mirror," I said. "What were you thinking we'd do with it?"

"I don't know. We might use it to signal someone if we can see that highway through the trees." She smoothed out her pants and said more softly, "Maybe I read too many Nancy Drew books as a kid."

"You seem too young to've had those books."

"My aunt had a collection, and I devoured them whenever we visited."

Another side to Addy. I knew we had little time for this conversation, but it felt so normal, so right.

"All right, people, what have we got?" We gathered around Lila, doing a last-minute check before we left the van for good. I had the lug wrench, keeping the other arm free to help Lila. She had her pocketbook and the walking stick. That left Addy carrying our supplies – the remaining water bottles and granola bars, the twine we'd pulled from the backpack, and the mirror. She'd found a large litter bag in the van and used some of the twine to fashion a strap so she could wear the bag on her shoulder.

"Wait," I said. "Lila, do you still have that lipstick in your purse?"

"I do, but what on earth are you thinking?" She dug it out and handed it to me, frowning the whole time like she thought I would do something juvenile.

I opened the driver's door, stepped up onto the sill and wiped the windshield clear of soot. In big block letters I wrote, "3 PEOPLE. WALKING SOUTH."

Satisfied, I stepped down to return the lipstick. Rather than looking pleased, both Lila and Addy were shaking their heads.

"What? Don't you think it's a good idea? If someone comes this way, they'll know where to look for us."

"Oh, it's a good idea alright, Joseph, but how about you change that number to a 5?"

I let out a breath. Jimmy and Eve. Were they really so far out of my thoughts? Or did I figure they were on their own now, so the hell with them? I stepped back up onto the door sill, smudged out part of the 3 and made it into a 5.

The three of us must've looked like a bunch of bums. Ripped and dirty clothes. Badly in need of a shower. Hobbling along in the middle of the road.

We weren't the same people we'd been yesterday. We were the Pineys now.

Chapter Thirty-One

How many miles could we walk in an hour? That useless thought occurred to me, even though I had no sense of distance or time. The day was still gray, if anything, even darker than it'd been. But it couldn't be dusk yet.

None of us spoke. I could feel my heartbeat pulsing in my ears. Walking didn't come easy for me. Not that my legs were weak. Hell, I could lift rocks and heft a wheelbarrow filled with mortar mix all day. But I was tired and my feet were sore. I'm sure it was no easier for Addy, and certainly not for Lila. No one complained.

The road curved in places, but to my eyes, it all looked the same – pine trees on both sides, no telephone poles or electric wires, no signs of life.

The wind picked up. I could feel it blowing against my back. If it was blowing the forest fire our way, we were at least heading away from it, and not toward it. I kept repeating that thought, convincing myself we were doing the right thing. And I kept looking for another road, even a dirt road leading to the right, something that

197

would take us in the direction where we'd heard that loud car and truck. Was it really just earlier today?

Lost in thought, I was jarred back to reality by a strange noise approaching from behind. I got a better grip on the lug wrench and spun around, ready for a fight.

A large buck and three small does were running down the road, heading right at us. I couldn't take it in at first, it was such a strange sight. "Get behind me!" I positioned myself to shield Addy and Lila. The deer raced by on either side, white tails up, paying as little notice of the three of us as they would a boulder in the road. The smell of animal musk swept over me. The smell of fear.

The deer weren't charging. They were escaping.

Addy grabbed my arm. "This is bad, Joe. What are we going to do? We can't walk any faster."

The wind was hot and dry. I couldn't see flames or feel heat from the fire, but dirty clouds of smoke billowed above the treetops. At ground level, the air was thick, the smell of burning pine strong.

I was trying to come up with a better plan when an explosion echoed in the distance. A dark column of smoke rose into the sky, black and oily. I had no doubt what had happened.

"That was our van, Joseph." Lila put a hand on my shoulder. "There's no going back now."

Anything I was about to say was interrupted by the sharp snap of fracturing glass. The plastic litter bag Addy had rigged into a knapsack split open, and the mirror – our "Nancy Drew" signaling device – hit the pavement.

I picked it up and saw my face reflected in a web of cracks. "Well, what the hell then!" I blurted out. With the sun hiding behind the clouds and no flashlight, I wasn't sure how we'd signal anyone anyhow.

"Shit, shit, shit." Addy spat out the words.

As course as my tongue is, I was still shocked to hear her swear.

"It doesn't matter, honey." Lila took hold of Addy's hands.

"I know it shouldn't, I know, but that superstition – seven years of bad luck ..." She burst into tears.

How did Addy's religion square with this old wives' tale? Italians have plenty of crazy notions about curses and bad luck. But God-will-forgive-you Addy? I guess we were all on edge. While Lila consoled Addy, I pitched the mirror into the woods.

"Why'd you do that?" Lila gave me a stern look.

I was exasperated. Was she questioning my judgment? "It was all cracked to hell. No use to us now."

Lila ignored me and kept trying to calm Addy. I wanted to do something to help, but I felt like a *ragazzo goffo* – a big, clumsy oaf next to the two women.

"Come on, Adelaide. Let's get our act together. We have to get out of here."

I picked up the granola bars and shoved them in my pockets, then gave Lila the water bottles. Her pocketbook was big enough to hold them. When Lila bent to retrieve her walking stick, I saw her grimace. "Should you take that other pill now? Are you going to make it alright?"

She practically snarled at me. "Don't you worry

about me, big boy! I'll make it alright. Let's just keep going."

I doubt she was trying to start a fight. It was probably Lila's pride talking. We continued down the road, heading to some place, any place, away from danger.

The fire – or the threat of it – was always right behind us. The road ahead was featureless – black pavement strewn with dead pine needles and gray sand, with woods on either side. It was like a nightmare where you're moving down a long hallway, but you never get closer to the door at the end.

People have told me that when you smell something bad, something really foul, after a while you get used to it, and you don't even notice it anymore. Bullshit. The stink from the burning pines was everywhere. I could feel it in the back of my throat. Taste it, too. I wanted to spit but my mouth was too dry. And my eyes stung. I tried not to wipe them. That would only make it worse. At least the wind had died down. But as Eve had told us, a forest fire can create its own weather.

I don't know how much time passed before we reached a fork in the road. To the left, the road was wider, with a yellow line painted down the center. To the right was the same unmarked macadam we'd been on. Neither one looked familiar. Neither one had any signposts.

"That's probably the way to Batsto," Addy said,

pointing to the left. "At least it's a bigger road. Isn't that better?"

I shook my head. "But if we're heading south and we want to get to the state highway, we need to go right."

I stared at Addy, and she gave me back as good as she got. Was this going to be a battle of wills? I was so damned tired, but I knew our choice could be critical.

"For God's sake, people, make up your minds!" Lila's voice was hoarse. She must have been exhausted.

"I know the wider road looks more promising," I said, "and it may well lead to Batsto. But that's just going deeper into the Pines. We've got to get away from all these trees. If there's someone who can help us, if there's anyone out there who isn't totally *pazzo*, that's where we'll find them." I flung my right arm out. "And that's where they'll find us."

Addy looked left and then right. I could almost see the wheels turning in her head. "I pray you're right, Joe."

"We can use your prayers right now," Lila whispered. She seemed defeated, smaller somehow.

"Okay, let's go." I tried to sound confident, convinced I was making the right decision, but I wasn't that sure. I'd just hoped I was. And I was fine with Addy's prayers. As they say, there are no atheists in foxholes.

We came upon a black-water lake alongside the road. Stubby, rotting tree trunks rose above the surface, remnants of some time in the past when this area must have been dry. At least all that water could be a buffer against the fire.

Swirling strands of mist crept across the road. The sight of all that moisture should have cheered me, but it was too easy to imagine weird shapes in the mist, waiting to ambush us.

Even though we were dead tired, we picked up our pace, trudging past that creepy lake. The mist seemed to follow us, dragged along by our feet. The road was still narrow, with trees forming a canopy overhead. And the soot and smell of burning pine never let up. I kept looking for an opening ahead, some sign that we'd made the right choice coming this way...that *I'd* made the right choice.

Addy saw the headlights first. "Joe! Lights. Up ahead." The car approached slowly, the low rumble of its engine producing an uneven rhythm, as if it would stall at any moment.

The car came to a stop before it reached us. It was old, some kind of Chevy station wagon from the '50s or '60s. But even in the mist and smoke, its bright blue and white two-tone paint and chrome wheels shone. This was no ordinary Chevy.

The driver's door opened and a big guy stepped out, keeping the door as a shield between us. He spoke to someone inside, but I couldn't understand what he'd said. The passenger door sprung open, and a little guy jumped out and sprinted toward us. "Joe? Joe!"

How the hell did he know my name?

He rushed me, and I gripped the lug wrench tighter. My God, I couldn't believe what I was seeing. The black jacket. The baseball cap. "J.J.?"

The lug wrench clattered to the road as he gave me a bear hug. *"¡Estás vivo!"* he said. "Not dead, Joe!"

Lila and Addy gathered closer. I saw the shock in Lila's eyes. But Addy had a strange smile on her face. She raised her arms to the sky. "Praise the Lord!" she said. "Praise the Lord, you're among the living!"

"But you were shot. We buried you." I'm not sure if I said it out loud or just in my head. J.J. released me and turned to Lila, who wrapped her arms around him, the little guy lost in her bosom. Soon we were all hugging him, practically smothering him with our embraces, reassuring ourselves that this was really him. That he was really alive.

"Come on, you guys, get in the car." The driver motioned to us. "I've got more strays to collect. *Vamos!*"

Lila was still silent. She tossed her improvised cane to the side of the road and hobbled toward the car. J.J. rushed to help her.

I grabbed hold of Addy's arm. "But how? I mean...Eve...the gun." I couldn't get the words out.

She shook her head. Her face looked almost blissful. "The Lord moves in mysterious ways, Joe."

All I could think was, *that's it?* J.J.'s alive, some other guy's dead, and we just thank God and move on?

I let go of her and watched as she walked away. My feet felt like they were cemented to the pavement.

Neil MacNeill

Chapter Thirty-Two

"It's a Chevy Nomad, isn't it? '55 or '56?" Addy seemed as excited about the car as she was about being rescued. We were crammed into the back seat, Addy behind the driver, who'd introduced himself as Miles, and J.J. straddling the transmission tunnel between us. Lila was up front, where she could stretch out her bum leg. The engine was so loud it was hard to make out what anyone was saying.

"Yup, these two-door Chevy wagons are pretty collectible." Miles grunted as he worked the steering wheel back and forth, turning his car back around in the narrow lane. I looked over my shoulder to check for signs of the fire, but all I could see was gray ash drifting down from the overcast sky. Maybe I should have felt relieved to be rescued, but my head was exploding. I looked at J.J.'s smiling face and kept seeing a bullet hole in his cheek and blood all over him. How could he be here, alive, well?

Lila turned in her seat to talk to J.J. "Did you see James and Evelyn?"

J.J.'s face scrunched up in a frown. "Jimmy. Eve. Not with you?"

"They left us," Lila said. "Early this morning." She shook her head. "Was it just this morning?"

"To hell with them," I muttered. "What about the guy we buried in the woods? Who was *he*? And what have we done?" No one paid attention to me.

Miles spoke above the engine's roar. "Your buddy J.J. had me driving all over these Podunk roads looking for you. I picked him up on Route 206 this morning. He didn't just wave me down – he stood in front of my car, forcing me to stop. And he was pretty damn insistent we find you." Miles looked at J.J. in the rearview mirror. "*¡Pero qué terco eres!* You're a stubborn SOB."

J.J. blushed. I don't know why he looked embarrassed. He'd probably saved our lives.

Miles downshifted and swerved to get past an abandoned pickup truck. We didn't have any seatbelts in back, so the three of us were shoved together. The seats looked newly upholstered, but the interior still had that musty old-car smell. And now that we were all in an enclosed space, the stench of smoke, sweat and dirty clothes gave me a headache.

"How'd you get this car running?" Addy shouted to the back of Miles's head. "I mean, all our electronics are fried."

"Ha! That's because most of the dorks in our club put in electronic ignitions. Not me. I've got a good old-fashioned dual-point distributor in this baby. And I'm probably one of the few guys around who knows how to set it up."

I tuned out their car talk. All I kept telling myself was that J.J. was alive. We hadn't buried him. Eve hadn't shot him. But who *had* she shot? Who *had* we buried? Was I the only one thinking about this?

"Lila!" I reached forward and grabbed her shoulder. "What about the other guy? What are we going to do?"

She shifted her body to get a better look at me. Her eyes glistened. "There'll be time for that, Joseph. Not now." She lowered her voice and I'm not sure I caught her next words. She seemed to say, "...time to think of ourselves."

Miles crept down the narrow road at a ridiculously slow pace. Maybe he was trying to avoid running over fallen branches with his precious Chevy, or he was watching out for deer and other animals spooked by the fire.

We were quiet for a while, caught up in our inner thoughts. Lila broke the silence, and she sounded more like herself. "And where exactly are you taking us, Mr. Miles?"

"Hey, lady, show some gratitude for your knight in shining armor here!" He patted his chest.

I couldn't see Lila's face, but I could imagine her expression. "Okay, *Mister* Miles." She spoke in a measured tone, emphasizing each syllable. "Thank you, *sir*!" She repeated her question with more force. "Now, where the heck are you taking us?"

"You're welcome, lady!" Miles didn't answer her right away, and I could tell Lila was losing her patience. Once we were on a more-or-less open stretch of road, he spoke to us again. "There's a small hospital outside

Hammonton. It's become a refugee center for all you lost souls. The state police helped set it up with volunteers from town. They also helped the guys in our club gas up our old cars. And they told us to go out and pick up anyone who wants to be rescued, people like you who are truly stranded." He ran a hand over the steering wheel like he was petting the family dog. "The only cars running are like mine – not a microchip in it!"

His comment snapped me out of my brooding, and I realized we still had no idea what had sparked this whole nightmare. "Was it really some kind of electronic pulse?"

"Pulse?" Miles glanced back at me. "What do you mean?"

"But everything's dead – you said it. Our electronics are useless. I heard...I mean, someone said it was some kind of electromagnetic pulse."

"Ha! That's as good an explanation as any." He blipped the throttle to downshift and swung around a utility pole leaning into the road.

"Well, what do *you* think happened? What have you heard?"

"You want to hear what I've heard? Okay. I was talking to an orderly at the hospital, and he said this was a pre-planned blackout, a military coup, and the President's been arrested for pedophilia. Another guy, a clerk at the police barracks, told me he was following some threads on social media before everything stopped, and this was the 'great reset,' whatever that means, and we had to get ready to fight Bill Gates and the elites. Bill Gates – right!" He let out a sharp breath, a cough or a laugh, I couldn't tell. "So, *you* decide what you want to believe."

"Have you seen..." Addy was hesitant. "Have people...disappeared?"

"What?" Miles angled the rearview mirror to get a better look at Addy. I'm not sure how he caught on so quickly. Maybe he saw the cross around her neck. "Oh, you mean like the Rapture? The End Times? That's another good one." He shook his head. "Plenty of accidents, fires, injuries of all kinds, and a few fatalities, from what I've heard, but no one's disappeared. I'm sure some people are missing. There's no way to tell right now."

"Huh." Addy sounded disappointed. Like Miles said, you decide what you want to believe.

Lila chimed in. "There has to be a logical explanation for all of our electronics suddenly stopping," she said. "Sorry, but I just can't go down that road – all those conspiracy theories, not to mention the Book of Revelations."

"Yeah, I'm with you, lady," Miles said. "But I haven't sorted out what that logical explanation is. Old machines ... like my Chevy here ... they're okay, if you can find gas to get them running, that is. Thank God the cops got a couple of old generators going at the barracks. And they've got their own gas tanks, so that's how I'm getting around."

"So, how is it out there?" Lila asked. "Are people ... behaving?"

Miles rubbed the back of his head, rolling his neck like he was working out a kink. "Some people are being good Samaritans. They're really helping out. Others are, you know, batshit crazy."

Addy leaned forward to talk into Miles's ear. "You said there were volunteers running this small hospital you're taking us to. What about the local churches? Are they helping people out?"

"There's some kind of evangelical church a couple blocks from the hospital," Miles said. "I saw some people milling around there." He paused. "I'm Catholic, so I don't know much about those Bible thumpers." He looked at Addy in the mirror again. "Sorry. No offense meant."

I waited to see how Addy would take that. She held her tongue. Maybe she didn't want to upset our "knight in shining armor."

The road widened, and we came to a stop sign at the highway. Miles wiped his forehead with a sleeve and turned to speak to us. "Look. Anything can happen on our way to the refugee center in Hammonton ... the hospital," he said. "Lots of ditched cars and crap on the road. Maybe some people doing crazy things to flag me down. Like I said, I'm supposed to pick up folks who are in danger, people who really need help, like you guys. But we've got to be careful. You never know if they're good guys or bad guys, if you know what I mean. But I promise I'll get you to safety."

He made a sharp left turn, rear tires squealing against the hard concrete of Route 206.

Chapter Thirty-Three

Pla-donk ... pla-donk ... pla-donk. I can still hear the sound of the car going over the expansion joints in the concrete roadway as we drove south toward Hammonton. The regular rhythm and gentle porpoising of the car lulled me into a light sleep. I have strong memories of what I saw, looking out from the car, like I'm replaying old movies in my head. Or maybe I dreamt them. At this point, I really don't know. But they're so vivid, so clear.

A blackened utility pole, its transformer splayed open, like something powerful had escaped from inside. Two young women riding bareback on a horse, galloping across the road in front of us, hellbent on getting somewhere, or getting away from someone. A grown man on a kid's bike, towing a little red wagon piled with bottled water and canned goods. An old farmhouse with a 4 x 8 sheet of plywood nailed to the mailbox, "Keep Out!" scrawled on it in black paint.

I was jarred to my senses when Miles jammed on the brakes and veered onto the shoulder to get around a jackknifed tractor-trailer. Once back on the road, he accelerated through the gears.

"Why are you driving so fast?" Lila yelled over the howl of the V8 engine.

"I'm not driving fast. I just don't want to stay in one place too long. Look, do you see anyone else on the road? Plenty of dead cars and trucks, all their advanced electronics not worth shit. This Chevy of mine is priceless right now." A manic look appeared on his face. "Some people might even kill to get their hands on it."

As we got closer to town, there were more houses on either side. We passed a deserted convenience store, its glass windows and doors smashed in, trash and food wrappers scattered all over. In the parking lot, three men huddled around a trash-can fire, cooking hotdogs on sticks. One of them smiled and waved, like we'd just driven past a bunch of friends enjoying a barbecue. How could it be that some people turned inward, expecting the worst from their neighbors, while others pitched in, making the most of the crazy situation?

We slowed to a crawl at an intersection with another highway. I think it was Route 30, one of the back ways to the Jersey shore.

I've only seen one of the Mad Max movies, but this looked pretty close to life imitating art – a black SUV rammed into the undercarriage of a delivery van that had flipped on its side, a red sports car wedged under the rear bumper of a landscaping truck, a big sedan so badly burned it was almost unrecognizable. Kernels of glass, shredded tires, and shards of plastic were scattered all over the intersection.

"Gotta go overland." Miles shifted into first gear and eased his wagon up a low curb and drove over a long patch of grass before getting back onto the pavement. Now, with fewer obstacles on the next stretch of road, he picked up speed. He glanced at us in the rearview mirror. "I need to warn you. There are only a few places that are safe. The hospital. Some churches. The state police barracks. Other than that, I don't know. Once I drop you off, don't go wandering."

We passed a large lake on the right, and I saw a blue "H" sign up ahead. If the hospital was a safe haven, I was ready for it – knackered, drained. *Spossata*. Not sure what to do next.

We pulled under the canopy near the ER entrance. The doors were jammed open with a pile of rocks. Inside, emergency lights cast yellow circles on the floor and walls. The silhouettes of people going back and forth seemed so normal, so orderly. It was a far cry from what I'd seen on the ride south.

Miles jumped out of the car and came around to help Lila. I reached down to find the release lever and pushed on the driver's seatback. The rest of us clambered out. Addy ran inside and soon emerged with a wheelchair. Ignoring Lila's complaints – "Oh, I can manage, Adelaide" – Addy settled her into the chair and wheeled her inside.

A burly cop wearing a heavy black vest stepped out

of the shadows, turning his head right and left, scanning the scene. I couldn't see his eyes behind dark sunglasses, but I was sure he paused when he saw me. I felt naked, exposed.

His right hand rested on his sidearm, like some hombre in a Sergio Leone western. I looked down at the pavement, forcing myself to avoid eye contact. But when I looked up, he was tilting his head, like he was trying to get a better look.

"Hey!" he called out. A trickle of sweat rolled down my back. "Is that you, Miles?"

"Yo, Officer Marinucci!" Miles sauntered over to chat with him. It took a good while for my heartbeat to slow down. Even though the two of them were soon deep in conversation, I still felt the cop's eyes on me, like I was a teenager hiding a six-pack his buddies had shoplifted.

I turned my back on them and walked over to J.J. He was leaning against the fender of the Chevy like he didn't have a care in the world. And I realized how much we owed him. If it wasn't for him, well, I'm not sure how things would have gone. "Thank you, J.J. *Gracias.*" That was about the extent of my Spanish. "We thought we'd lost you. We thought..."

J.J.'s gaze shifted over my shoulder, and I felt someone grab me from behind. I stiffened, then realized it was a hug, a warm, soft hug. Addy held me and whispered in my ear. "Thank God we're safe and out of the Pines." It was such a fleeting moment, one I sometimes replay when I think about Addy. One I wish had lasted longer.

I turned to her. "Thank God ...and J.J.," I said, trying

to make light of our intimacy. I didn't want to read too much into her embrace. As my Italian momma used to say, the oaths of lovers are like those of sailors.

"Joe, I've got to leave now."

"What? Where can you go? You heard Miles. Only a few places are safe around here."

She stared out over the hospital lot – a mishmash of parked cars and others that were stopped halfway between coming and going, frozen in place like someone had hit "pause" on a video. I could see a white church steeple in the distance.

"Yes, I heard him. That's why I'm going to that Evangelical church he mentioned. It's just a few blocks away."

I grabbed her shoulders, forcing her to look at me. "You can't just leave. We have to figure out what to do. All of us have to agree on this."

She pulled free and shook her head. "Life is for the living. Isn't that what they say? I need to help my fellow Christians do the Lord's work."

"Addy ..." I tried to find the words to make her understand. "Okay, you want to help people." I started to pace. I needed to take my time and say it right. "But what about the Hispanic guy Eve shot, the guy we thought was J.J.? He was someone, a son or maybe a father. Don't we owe him something? People need to know what happened to him. And we need to tell someone what we've done ... so they can dig up the body and identify him. We can't just walk away from that."

I saw a spark in her eyes. "I didn't see you going over to that policeman. You had plenty of opportunity.

What's stopping you?"

That really pissed me off. We were all in this together – Eve and Jimmy, Addy, Lila and me. Sure, Eve shot the guy, but we'd all covered him up – literally. How could I tell the cop if Addy didn't want me to? Lila had to agree, too. And what about Eve? It would turn her life upside down. I couldn't believe Addy was just going to leave and wash her hands of it all.

I lost it. My Italian temper, I guess. Things came out I wish I could take back. "Is it because he was Hispanic – probably illegal? So his life doesn't matter to you, is that it? And you call yourself a good Christian!"

Addy sucked in her breath. I could see I'd gone too far. "He's in God's hands now."

"Please, Addy. I'm sorry, sorry for what I said."

"I need to leave before it gets too dark." She turned away from me but glanced back. "God bless your soul, Joe."

I watched her walk into the gathering darkness, torn between running after her and biting my thumb at her.

The sound of rushing air, like a gale force wind gaining strength, made me turn and look into the sky. The sound grew, and I saw the shapes of two jet planes silhouetted against the setting sun. As they passed low overhead, the sound turned into a high-pitched whistle. They banked and headed north, disappearing over the treetops. People rushed out of the hospital, looking up and cheering. Miles pumped his fists into the air.

I walked over to Miles, who was slapping J.J. on his shoulder. "They're back!" he said. "It's going to be okay."

I squinted up at the sky – the jets were long gone and it was quiet now. "What does it mean, those jets? Why are you so excited?"

Miles looked at me like I was an *idiota*. "Don't you get it? Those were Maryland Air National Guard A-10 Thunderbolts. I could see the insignia on the vertical stabilizer. They're still flying! Whatever made everything stop didn't affect them down in Maryland. Maybe it's not widespread, or maybe they figured out a way around it. But it means this will all be over soon. We'll be okay."

"Yeah, I guess that makes sense." I rubbed my face and tried to get a grip.

Miles shrugged. "Cheer up, big guy. We're all going to get through this." He waited for a response, but I was too wrapped up in my emotions. "Anyhow, J.J. and I have to get going."

That brought me out of my daze. "What? I mean, where are you going?"

"I've got to report back to the police barracks before I head home." He turned to J.J., who was already getting into the car. "And J.J.'s got some relatives south of town." As if to make that point clear, he added, "There's a big Hispanic community there, and he said he wants to help them out."

Miles hopped into his hot-rod Chevy and fired up the engine, making almost as much noise as the jet fighters. J.J. rolled down his window, and I reached in to pat his shoulder.

"There's so much I want to say to you. I don't know how to begin."

J.J. just smiled and touched my arm. Miles leaned

over and yelled out to me. "See you on the flip side, amigo!" He raced the engine, put the shifter in gear and eased away from the hospital. Once he was out on the highway, he gunned it, accelerating hard. I watched until his taillights disappeared around the bend.

Chapter Thirty-Four

"Please fill in your name and address, and print clearly." The receptionist blocked my way into the hospital. They'd cordoned off access, so I had no choice but to deal with her before going further. She sat behind a large desk and had the kind of bored but superior expression you'd see at the DMV.

After everything that had just happened, after everything we'd all been through, the last thing I wanted to do was deal with some bureaucratic roadblock. "I just want to talk to Lila – the woman who was wheeled in here a moment ago."

She let out an exasperated sigh and repeated, "Please fill in your name and address."

I glanced down at her name tag – Reyna. "Here's the deal, Reyna. I'm not sure what I'm going to do next, if I'm going to spend the night here or what. I really need to talk to Lila. So, why don't you help me out and let me get by?"

Reyna pulled off her reading glasses and gave me a look. "As I assume you're aware," she said, sounding for all the world like one of the nuns from grade school, "we have no electricity, and as a result, no working computers. That means no electronic files. My job is to make sure no one goes in or out of this clinic without signing the register." She paused, maybe to make sure I understood. Like I had a choice. "And I take my job very seriously." She turned the register to face me and handed me a pen.

My frustration and fatigue were fighting with each other. Ultimately, fatigue won out. "Gotcha," I mumbled, and started to fill in the first open line in the register.

"And print clearly."

I almost scratched the pen across the page. I took a deep breath and continued writing. When I finished, she turned the register around, no doubt checking my handwriting. I had more flashbacks to elementary school. "So, do I get a passing grade?"

"It'll do," she said, not showing even the slightest smile at my remark. She unclipped the rope from a nearby stanchion and motioned me past.

"Where will I find ...?"

The words were barely out of my mouth when Reyna said, "There's a nurses' station halfway down the hall." This sure wasn't a warm welcome.

It didn't take me long to find Lila among the rows of hospital beds. The patients all around her seemed semi-conscious, at best. Lila was propped up with an IV in one arm and a large bandage around her leg. She looked drowsy, but perked up when she saw me. "Joseph! I'm so glad you're here. Come sit by me."

Pleated privacy curtains separated her from the beds on either side. There was just enough space for one metal chair next to her. I squeezed in, ruffling the curtains, and was greeted by a muffled complaint from whoever was in the next bed. So much for privacy.

I was eager to ask her how she felt about our ... situation ... but I kept my voice down so we wouldn't be heard. "We need to talk."

"We most certainly do. But where's Adelaide?"

After I filled in Lila on everything she'd missed, including my fight with Addy, I was even more drained. I kept trying to find a way to deal with what was weighing on me. They say Catholics are laden with guilt, but I hadn't been to Mass in years.

In the short time we'd been together in the Pines, I got to know Addy and Eve, and everyone else in our group, for that matter. Fate threw us together. Sometimes that led to attraction, like for Addy and me. And sometimes...

My Momma used to say that with some people, as soon as you meet them, you can feel the dirt under the rug. That's the way I felt with Jimmy right from the start.

Eve was a different story. After everything she'd gone through, I felt sorry for her. She wasn't evil. It wasn't a murder she'd committed. It was all a horrible accident. But we also had an obligation to whoever we'd buried in the woods. And to his family.

Whatever I'd decide to do would affect everybody. I couldn't do this on my own.

At one point, Lila closed her eyes. I thought she was dozing off, but she was just gathering her thoughts. "Before you go on, I need to tell you something," she said. "Maybe it will help you understand why I'm so hesitant."

"I'm not going anywhere." That brought a weak smile to her lips.

"When my son, Mark, was younger, he got into some trouble. I guess all teenagers do." She looked down, not meeting my eyes before continuing. "But this was gang-related."

I could see she was having a hard time getting this out. "It's okay, Lila, it's just between you and me."

"I know, Joseph, I know. So, of course, I did everything I could for him. Eventually, he got past it. But I'll never forget when my supervisor at the county office pulled me aside and said I'd better straighten that boy out – his exact words. He said it reflected badly on our office, and by extension, on the county commissioner."

She wiped her eyes and took a few deep breaths before continuing. "*It would reflect on the commissioner!* Like I could give a...oh, I shouldn't say what I'm thinking, Joseph. Hate is like a cancer, and I don't want it in my life."

I got up and moved to the foot of her bed, the only space big enough for me to walk and think. I had a devil on one shoulder and an angel on the other. On the one hand, we'd buried the poor bastard Eve had shot in the middle of nowhere. An unknown grave for an unknown man. And on the other, I kept hearing Addy's words at our make-shift grave – "to everything, there is a season."

I understood why Lila didn't want to get caught up in a police investigation, but we had to do something, say something to somebody. I went back to the hard metal chair by her bed.

"I get it. We have to consider...what we say. About what we did. And especially about Eve. I can't stop thinking about Eve and how she looked when she left us."

"Oh, my yes. That poor young child. She was broken by what happened."

"Dio ci aiuti!"

"What's that, Joseph? You know I don't understand your Italian."

"My Momma would say it often. It means, 'God help us.'"

A voice from the other side of the curtains broke into our conversation. "Amen to that, brother."

Fists clenched, I flung the curtain back to confront the S.O.B. who'd been eavesdropping on us. My temper ebbed when I looked down on the frail old guy in the next bed. He turned his head toward me, but he didn't look like he had enough strength to sit up.

"I'm sorry!" he said. "I didn't mean to intrude, but I couldn't help but hear you."

Now what do we do? I thought. "What did you hear?" I demanded. "Tell me."

"You were talking about Eve, that sad but oh-so-pretty young girl who was in here this morning." He chuckled. I couldn't imagine what he found so amusing.

I was dumbfounded, trying to figure out if the guy

was senile. Lila said what I was thinking. "You're talking nonsense, old man."

He coughed, but somehow kept smiling. "I heard you mention her name," he said. "Eve. The sad young blonde. With the great figure! She was in the same bed you're in."

Lila sat up straighter. "You're talking about Evelyn Jesko? Are you sure?"

"I'm not sure of much these days. But I know that a young woman named Eve was in that bed this morning. Or maybe it was around noon..."

Could it be? The old man seemed confused about the time, but he was pretty adamant about a woman named Eve. That's not a very common name. Jimmy and Eve left us early in the morning. It was dusk now. They *could* have made it to this hospital ahead of us.

"Was she with an Asian man named James Lim?" Lila asked.

"I don't remember anyone being with her. She was all alone, as far as I could tell. And she left so suddenly."

A thought struck me, and I rushed back down the hallway. Reyna was still there, doing her job as guard and record-keeper.

"You're back," she said in a manner-of-fact voice.

I tried to catch my breath. "Eve...a woman named Eve, Evelyn. Earlier today. I need to see your register."

She frowned. "That's not allowed. It's not a public document."

I raised my eyes to the heavens. *Ma dai!* Was she serious? "Eve, Evelyn, was part of our group. We were stuck in the Pine Barrens together. She left us earlier today. Please, you've got to help me. Is there an Evelyn Jesko in your register?"

After my rant, the smallest smile appeared on Reyna's face. "I can't show you the register," she said.

I was about to grab it from her.

"But I *can* tell you about Eve Jesko." Reyna paused, like she was weighing how much to say. "She came in here about midday. Seemed kind of out of it. That's not a medical diagnosis, I know, but I'm not a doctor." Again the pause.

"And? Where is she now?"

"She was only here about an hour or so. Then she left with one of the Dade boys."

"What are you telling me?" I closed my eyes, taking this all in. "She left with someone? Where did they go?"

Reyna frowned and shook her head. Maybe she finally realized how much this meant to me. "One of the Dade boys came around, riding on a motorcycle. It was so loud and disruptive, people came out to see what was going on. The Dades are a bad lot. They're always getting into trouble. Officer Marinucci went over to talk to him, but he just sneered. The kid probably had a six-pack in his saddlebag. That's the way they are, the Dade boys."

"And Eve?" I tried to keep my frustration in check.

"Well, Eve walked out like she was in a trance. I know one of our nurses had examined her and told me there was nothing wrong, medically. She was just, I don't know, out of it. And wouldn't you know it, she starts talking to that Dade kid. The next thing you know, the two of them roar off together on that motorcycle. It was probably stolen."

For once I kept my mouth shut, waiting for Reyna to say more.

"I talked to Officer Marinucci after they'd left, but he said that under the circumstances, there was nothing we could do."

"Nothing we could do," I mumbled.

Reyna shook her head. That was all I was going to get out of her.

I trudged back to Lila's bed, more weary and confused than ever.

Chapter Thirty-Five

The next few days were a blur. The hospital was a safe haven, a place to treat people who needed it, a place for those of us who had nowhere else to go. Old school buses seemed to be the only vehicles running. Other than classic cars like the one Miles brought us here in. Civilization was returning in slow stages, but there was still no electricity. And no outside help. I guess the government had its hands full in the cities. A little town in South Jersey didn't matter much.

I stayed with Lila as she got better, and once or twice I tried to find Addy at the nearby church. A helpful woman there said Addy had joined some parishioners delivering food to survivors in the neighborhood. I left a message for her, but never heard back.

It was on the third day, I think, that I got a ride to Chester in an old school bus, heading up Route 206. I figured I could find my way home to Middle Valley from there. A doctor suggested Lila stay another day. She had a slight fever, and they were concerned about her diabetes. We had no idea when telephone service would return, but Lila and I exchanged numbers.

The ride back north didn't go easy. At one point, near Bordentown, a pile-up of cars blocked the road. We couldn't get around it. The bus driver started to back up, but then stopped and shut off the engine. He told us he would try to find help, and he walked away. Like Miles with his hot-rod Chevy, I assumed the driver was a volunteer, and I didn't have a lot of confidence I'd ever see him again.

We ended up spending the night there, sleeping on the bus. That sure as hell gave me flashbacks to my night in the Pines. Yeah, we weren't stuck in the middle of the woods. I could see houses in the distance, all dark. That meant more people, and that meant greater odds that some lunatic was going to force his way onto the bus for who knows what. I wasn't the only one who was restless. People talked in whispers well into the night. I woke up at one point and heard a scream, not sure if it came from me or someone else.

The next morning, our driver did show up, and he'd brought along a local wrecker service, a guy with an ancient GMC truck. They pulled some cars out of the way, and we continued our trip north.

The bus didn't make it all the way to the center of Chester. There were too many dead cars and trucks blocking the intersections. The driver dropped us off on the outskirts of town, and we all headed off in different directions.

I walked toward home – it was only about 8 miles – stopping from time to time to rest. I saw a few people milling about in the middle of Long Valley, so I ducked into a side street to avoid them. Who knows what they might have done? I couldn't trust strangers any more. I'm ashamed to admit I stole a bike that was leaning against a garage.

When I finally got home, it was just getting dark again.

Everything seemed normal when I stepped inside my back door. Except for the silence, that is. You don't realize how much background noise all our appliances and electronics make until they stop. It was cold inside – my old oil burner needed electricity as much as any modern contraption – but it was manageable. I dug out some warm clothes and bundled up.

The food in the fridge was spoiled, of course. And what a smell! I made do with cans of tuna and a bottle of Chianti. The next day, or maybe it was the day after, power came on for a few minutes before browning out again.

Even though I knew telephone service wouldn't be any more reliable than electricity, I found an old landline phone in the basement and plugged it in. When I checked for a dial tone, it was as silent as the rest of the house.

So it was a real jolt, about a week later, when the phone rang. The line crackled, but Lila's voice was unmistakable.

"Joseph, is that you?"

"Yes! Lila, it's so good to hear from you."

For a moment, I thought she'd been disconnected, but I could still hear static on the line. "I have some bad news, Joseph."

What could be worse than all the dead and injured from this event? This catastrophe that struck the Mid-Atlantic states like a bolt out of the blue? "What is it, Lila? What happened?"

"It's Evelyn. She's dead."

I almost dropped the phone. I sat down hard on the floor, the long cord from the phone stretched to its limits. "How?"

"It was a motorcycle accident. I heard from a friend of mine, a state trooper."

"Are they sure? What ... what happened?"

Lila took a deep breath. "Give me a minute." I heard the phone clunk down on a hard surface, and Lila blowing her nose. My mind was racing.

"Are you still there, Joseph?"

"Yes. Yes, Lila. What happened to Eve? Tell me."

"The trooper called it a one-vehicle accident. She and that young man she was with on the motorcycle skidded off the road, somewhere near Bordentown. They hit some trees. They weren't wearing helmets or anything. He said they probably died quickly, if that's any consolation. It must have happened the same day they left that hospital."

"God rest their souls," I said. My religious upbringing was surfacing again. It took me a moment to voice my next thoughts. "And Jimmy? Did your trooper friend know anything about him? Did you ask?"

"Yes, Joseph, I asked. He said he'd look into it, but the police have hundreds of people they're trying to locate. It's going to take weeks before we can do some searching on our own. I hate to admit it, but I miss

Google."

"So, we don't know how he and Eve got separated down in the Pines." I said it more to voice my thoughts than to ask the question. "And now, we may never know."

We were both silent, listening to the interference on the telephone line.

"Does this change things for us now?" I asked. "You know, with what Eve did?"

"I'm sorry to say that it doesn't change things for me, Joseph. I can't get involved. I could lose my job. As it is, I'm not sure when I'll be able to go back to work. When the office will open. I don't have much savings." She let that sink in. "Do you understand?"

"Dio ci aiuti!"

"Yes, Joseph, God help us all."

By Christmas, most of the things we take for granted were back – power, heat and water. The massive federal and state aid certainly helped.

Some time in January, I got a Christmas card from Addy. It took me a while to open it. When I did, there wasn't much inside other than a "God bless you, Joe," and a note that said she'd moved back to her hometown in Virginia.

Neil MacNeill

Chapter Thirty-Six

People make easy judgments. They think the world is no more complicated than yes or no. You're either saved or you're going straight to hell. You're either telling the truth or you're a liar. You're either innocent or...

Is there really that much distance between innocence and guilt? Most would say they're a long way apart, opposite ends of some moral straight line. But I think they're much closer. There's a gray and rocky place between them. It's the land of the word "but." People don't want to go there. And for those of us who do, it's like walking into the deep woods where paths go in many directions. You could get lost there. Some of us do.

For days after Lila's call, I kept waiting for a knock on the door, or a call from the police. I think it's a Biblical saying – "the truth will out." Even with the hundreds of deaths in New Jersey and surrounding states that October, even with so many missing – people still unaccounted for – eventually someone would try to find out what happened to the man Eve shot. The man we buried in the Pines.

But one day led to another. People got on with their lives. Everyone seemed to put all this in the past, to forget it ever happened.

I haven't gotten a call from Lila in a long time now, or a Christmas card from Addy, for that matter. I guess we really didn't want to stay in touch. It would only trigger all the memories of what happened seven years ago, what we did in the Pines. It's easier to sweep it under the rug, to forget, if we can.

Seven years. All that time and other than my daughter, this is the first I've told anyone about all this. Do I feel remorse, guilt? Yeah, almost every day. But I haven't done anything about it.

I haven't gone to the police. I should have done that long ago, no matter the consequences for Lila, Addy and me. Time passed and life went back to normal, and well, here I am. But I didn't want to take this to my grave. Hell, I even catch myself praying sometimes. I think Addy would be pleased.

Our decision, at least at first, was to save Eve. If the truth came out, it would have ruined her life. But she was dead. We knew that early on.

Lila and I had made a devil's bargain. We'd traded the comfort of our everyday lives – no scandals, no black marks against us – for the life of an unknown man. Of course, he wasn't unknown. Only to us. I was brought up to believe that all life is sacred. But that depends. Doesn't it?

The more time that passed, the less likely either of us would speak up. You can judge me for that. You probably should.

Before I walked into this room for this oral history, I had a good look around at this museum, this memorial. It's like a cathedral to atone for what happened in that instant when science and nature collided. To be honest, I'm surprised they built this place, or even admitted this is where it all started. But with all the dead and missing, I guess they had to do something.

I spent some time in the Hall of Remembrance, looking at the names projected on the walls. One side of the memorial was for the missing, the other for the dead. It was probably crazy, searching among the names of the missing for some Hispanic man, a name that might trigger a connection with the guy we buried. Of course, Eve's name was among those listed as dead.

You're probably wondering about Jimmy Lim. He's one of the hundreds of missing ... *still* missing. I saw his name projected on the wall with all the others.

It's a good memorial, I guess. But what do you get from it? All those missing people are probably dead. It's been too long to think otherwise. Some wandered off when their cars stopped, and maybe they ended up falling into a ditch or something. Some may have died of starvation or exposure. Some were probably killed.

I'm not much for poetry. If you're trying to say something, just say it – you don't need to rhyme. We had to memorize poems in school, and one was a favorite of

Sister Mary Elizabeth. The last line has stayed with me. I didn't understand what it was about when I was a kid. I think I do now. It ends with, "After the first death, there is no other."

Whoever you are, out there, buried in the Pines, *riposare in pace.*

Thank you for reading!

If you've enjoyed *A Stillness in the Pines,* please consider posting a review on Amazon and Goodreads, and letting your friends know about this book on social media. Ratings and reviews – even just a word or two – help draw in new readers.

With thanks,

Neil

Help Protect the Pine Barrens!

Please consider a donation to the Pinelands Preservation Alliance, a 501(c)(3) charitable organization (www.pinelandsalliance.org). Your donation supports their work to protect New Jersey's Pine Barrens, the largest wilderness on the East Coast between Maine and Florida. This amazing place is home to tree frogs, northern pine snakes and river otters. Its sandy roads, winding rivers and historic villages are enjoyed by people from all over our region and the world. The Pinelands Preservation Alliance's job is to make sure this special place remains protected. Your donation will help.

Acknowledgements

It takes a receptive group of friends to create a novel like *A Stillness in the Pines*. For biweekly reviews of each chapter, the Schooley's Mountain Writers' Critique Group was invaluable. Reyna Favis, Mark Christmas, Lauri Berg (who helped sort out the eventual title of the book), Emily Thompson, and David Chubb each provided a unique perspective. I greatly appreciate Reyna's help with the intricacies of independent publishing.

The Middle Valley Wordsmiths – Renny Hodgskin, Mark Kitchin, Charles Levin, D.J. Murphy, and Dave Watts – also shaped the narrative of this novel. I'm especially in debt to Charlie Levin for his marketing tips and ongoing encouragement. Eleanor Wagner also helped me promote my books online and at local events. When doubts or everyday roadblocks stymied progress, both groups of indie authors inspired me to continue.

Beyond my own research, I was fortunate to get help from many friends and associates with specialized knowledge: Alberto "Tico" Llaurador for J.J.'s Spanish conversations; Claudio Rietti and his Italian connections for Joe's Italian utterances; Lt. Col. Robert B. Post, USAF (Ret.), for help with aviation details; Miles Lamb, P.E., for engineering and firearms insights; and Chris Coddington and Dave Emmerling for help with cover design. The Italian phrases were difficult to sort out, since these vary by region and many have been highly modified by Italian-Americans.

My beta readers, Mandy Szigethy, Kathleen Berg, Mark Christmas, and Tommy Frkovich, helped me avoid last-minute pitfalls. When all is said and done, however, any remaining errors are mine alone. Finally and most sincerely, I thank my wife, Martha, for encouraging me ... and offering detailed proofreading comments.

My Italian-American Influences

My maternal grandmother's maiden name was Rosa Aromando. Such was the political climate when she and her siblings were young that her brother changed his last name to Armand to avoid discrimination. Grandmom was a proud woman, but she didn't talk much about her ancestry.

It was a different story with my Mom, who often talked about her Italian ancestors who "rode with Garibaldi." That meant little to me as a kid.

My real immersion into Italian-American culture came from Phil and Joe, carpenters who worked for my Dad. Phil, in particular, taught me many crude sayings that even Joe Scarapone would be embarrassed to repeat.

Growing up in South Jersey

A Stillness in the Pines is not an autobiography, but many of the novel's scenes and episodes were inspired by growing up in deepest South Jersey (not "down the Shore," but in a small town situated below the Mason-Dixon line). The "four boys" – my brother and cousins – would roam the woods on summer days, looking for Indian arrowheads, electrical insulators from some long-forgotten project, or if we were really lucky, a fragment of a plane that had crashed in the Pines. We would build tarpaper shacks or "mud huts" from whatever we could find or pilfer nearby. All manner of adventures awaited, just beyond our back doors. It was a time and place when our parents could send us off exploring in the woods without fear of lurking predators. When I was older, however, I did have a run-in with a Piney quite similar to one described by Joe Scarapone.

The Real Pineys

John McPhee's book, *The Pine Barrens*, was an inspiration for this novel. It was written decades ago, but the Piney culture he describes still rings true. Go back in time a bit further, and you can find "research" that claims Pineys were a separate species with "distinct morals and manners." In reality, Pineys are just ordinary people who live off the grid or at very least have as little to do with "outsiders" as possible. Some say that Pineys no longer exist. I disagree! Drive down some fire road deep in the Pine Barrens and you may come across one yourself. These are not ignorant or necessarily unlawful people. They just want to be left alone and apart from the rest of "civilized" New Jersey.

The Jersey Devil

Oh, my, where to begin? In my hometown, most people placed the origins of the Jersey Devil in Estellville, not Leeds Point. The legend, however, is universal – a half-man, half-demon who terrorizes local farmers and kills their livestock. There were many sightings of the Jersey Devil when I was growing up, and I recall newspaper accounts from as far afield as Chicago relating stories of people who swear they saw him. Some fierce, nocturnal animals certainly live in the Pines, including coyote and bobcats. These critters are likely responsible for the animal deaths blamed on the Jersey Devil. But like Bigfoot or other "mythical" creatures, we may never know the truth.

The Truth about EMPs

Electromagnetic Pulses are "a real and present danger." That was the conclusion of one expert who testified before a U.S. House of Representatives Committee on Homeland Security in 2014. According to the committee chair, "the consequences of such electromagnetic pulses could be devastating for many millions of people who would be left without access to potable water, food, bank accounts, medications, communications, transportation, and many other important electronically based activities."

Google the subject and you'll come across many similar comments from credible sources. And, by the way, Project Starfish Prime and the Soviet's Project K, as described by Jimmy Lim, were very real.

Automotive Realism

I'm a diehard automotive enthusiast, so I get quite upset when I see a car described incorrectly in a novel. I tried to avoid that pitfall. The old Ford 8N tractor that the Piney drove was a mainstay of many farmers until quite recently. It's now a valued collectible. The Mercedes-Benz Sprinter van that broke down in the Pines stretches the truth a bit – there is no diesel hybrid available (at least not yet). But I spent plenty of time looking at specs and photos so I could get the details of that van right. Finally, Miles's hotrod Chevy Nomad is a real gem that GM only produced for a few years. These two-door wagons are some of the coolest cars to come out of the '50s.

Questions for Discussion:
A Book Club Guide

1. Early in the novel, Joe Scarapone claims he's not a religious man. By the end of the story, his religious upbringing seems to play a larger role. Do you think he's ultimately seeking atonement? Can you empathize with his actions?

2. While Joe was not directly involved with a killing, he did play a role in "covering it up" (quite literally!). Peer pressure and group dynamics were involved with the decision to bury the body in the woods. Among the five characters, who do you feel is least to blame?

3. Throughout the novel, Addy's faith guides her actions. But once the body is "properly" buried, she seems to have reached peace with the group's decision not to reveal their secret. Do you agree with her actions? Do you think the events in the Pines changed her outlook?

4. Joe and Addy have a genuine attraction for each other, but there's always something that comes between them. In other circumstances, do you think the two of them could have continued or even built on their relationship?

5. What do you think happened to Jimmy Lim? Do you think Eve was involved with his disappearance?

6. We never find out exactly who was killed and buried in the Pines, but it's implied that the man was a Hispanic immigrant, and likely undocumented. Given the scale of the EMP catastrophe, how much effort do you think would have been made to find missing persons who had no other connections, no relative to seek them out? Do you think this is a cynical outlook or close to reality?

7. Lila is described as the group's "North Star," someone who appears to be a very ethical and fair-minded individual. Yet she resists telling the authorities about what happened in the Pines. Given her history with her son and her concerns for her job, how do you feel about her decision? What would you do in her place?

An Excerpt from *Exit Row*

If you enjoyed this story, you might consider my first novel, *Exit Row*. Here's an excerpt:

48 Drury Lane, Seaford, England
Sunday, September 15, 1991 • 9:03 p.m.

He awoke again, and turned to look at the clock.

21:03. What the...crazy...okay, 21 minus 12...is nine. Nine...at night.

He rose slowly, aware of the pain in his head and stiffness in his limbs, but more determined now.

This is absurd...this isn't happening. He willed a stop to his stream of consciousness, trying to control his breathing and clear his mind. But then a low rumbling from his stomach ruined his concentration. *I've got to find some food.*

He looked around at the bed, the dull green walls and thin window glass with peeling paint overlapping from the frame onto the glazing. *What a drab room.*

Reaching across the covers, he found the room keys. *Money. The bag...*

He opened the black briefcase, still lying at the foot of the bed, and pulled out the roll of currency. *It seems I have money.* He pulled out two £20 notes and placed the rest of the wad back inside the briefcase, then turned to look outside. Streetlights and a bright half-moon illuminated the rooftops.

I wonder if it's cold out. He looked down at his clothes — khaki pants with mud on the cuffs, brown loafers in need of a shine, a light-blue long-sleeve shirt. He opened the briefcase again and pulled out the wool cap. *Nice cap.*

Walking out into the hall, he turned to lock the door to Number 11. For a moment he stared at the tarnished brass number plate on the door. Then he pocketed the keys, tucked the cap into the back of his waistband and headed down the hall to the stairway. His movements were stiff and slow.

The small city park was mostly deserted, with just a few couples strolling hand in hand, and one or two people walking their dogs. Johnny McEllwain stood under a streetlamp, smoking a cigarette, looking up and down the street. As a man approached, walking a German Shepherd, Johnny stubbed out his cigarette and waited for him to come closer.

The man looked at Johnny, looked down at the sidewalk, and then walked just behind him, leading his dog to urinate on a nearby bush. Without looking up, the man said, "It must be raining in Dublin."

"Why don't we just cut the crap, Eddie?" Johnny replied.

"Don't use my name!" the man hissed.

"Look, Eddie, I want some answers, and I'm not going to play your cloak-and-dagger games tonight."

Eddie sighed, and looked nervously around him. "Right, Johnny, so what's troubling you tonight?"

"I need to know if it was our doing. Were we behind it?"

"I'm sure I don't know what you're going on about," Eddie said.

"Damn it all, Eddie!" Johnny blurted out, then much softer, "The plane crash, that's what. Were we behind it?"

Eddie looked around again. "I wish to Christ you'd be a bit more circumspect. You never know who's around." He paused. "No, Johnny, if you have to know, we wouldn't be able to engineer something like that. We have some plans, big plans, but nothing as, well, as spectacular as a jetliner falling from the sky. Now then, does that make you feel better?"

After a moment, "Yes, I suppose it does." He paused again. "I…sometimes I just don't know what I'm playing at here. That's all."

"You're playing an important role, Johnny, a vital role." Eddie looked up and down the now-deserted street and grabbed Johnny's elbow. "In fact, we've moved up our plans by a week. We need your help. And we may need more help besides, if you catch my drift. Walk with me a bit and let's talk."

The two men and the dog walked off together into the cover of the night.

 Exit Row is available on Amazon, in print or as an e-book
Click the code to go to Amazon.com

About the Author

Neil MacNeill is the penname of Neil MacNeil Szigethy, an award-winning copywriter of advertising, marketing and sales training materials. Neil grew up in a small town on the edge of the Pine Barrens, and spent many childhood summers exploring fire roads and moss-covered ruins with his brother and cousins. He currently lives in New Jersey with his wife, Martha. *A Stillness in the Pines* is his second novel.

You can reach the author at:
NeilMacNeill.books@gmail.com.

A Stillness in the Pines

Neil MacNeill

Made in the USA
Middletown, DE
20 May 2023